Cayuga Secon(
F BER
Berlingieri, J.M. The right to b
T 2267
MW01119808

THE RIGHT TO BEAR ARMS AND METE JUSTICE

BOOK I: THE KNIGHT

Joseph Mario Berlingieri

CAYUGA SECONDARY SCHOOL
LIBRARY

PUBLISH AMERICA

PublishAmerica
Baltimore

© 2007 by Joseph Mario Berlingieri.
All rights reserved. No part of this book may be reproduced, stored in a retrieval system or transmitted in any form or by any means without the prior written permission of the publishers, except by a reviewer who may quote brief passages in a review to be printed in a newspaper, magazine or journal.

First printing

This is a work of fiction. Names, characters, places, and incidents either are the product of the author's imagination or are used fictitiously. Any resemblance to actual persons, living or dead, events, or locales is entirely coincidental.

ISBN: 1-4241-8348-0
PUBLISHED BY PUBLISHAMERICA, LLLP
www.publishamerica.com
Baltimore

Printed in the United States of America

In the name of God
St. Michael and St. Zorren
I give you the right to
Bear arms and mete justice
In the land.
It is your duty to vanquish
Ignorance, oppression and selfishness.
Words of Old

One need only look to children to aspire to acts of heroism.

J.M.B.

Book I: The Knight is a story that follows the rise of a young hero named Brandyn, who comes from the Wendover Lowlands. By a strange turn of fate, he becomes immersed into a world of high adventure.

Although Brandyn is incorruptible, he is full of delusions about slaying dragons and rescuing damsels in distress. He is rudely awakened when he learns of the treachery in the king's court. He is forced to stand up to the wickedness and restore order, but he makes a powerful enemy.

Brandyn also realizes that he has fallen in love with a beautiful girl from Wendover, but his enemy, the ambitious Lucio, learns this and plots against him.

The challenges he faces as a squire, and the crisis that ensues when he is knighted, will lead Brandyn away from his homeland and true love.

BOOK I: THE KNIGHT

Beginnings

In a time not long ago, the passing years saw the commitment to truth and justice become an ideal that faded to memory and make-believe. An all-powerful God came to replace the smaller gods, yet old habits were not easily forgotten. Although the people had embraced this new theology, it was cynicism that replaced hope in these dark times. When the path was laden with difficulty, the people turned to the smaller gods for help. The people had forgotten to count their blessings, and when that happens, even the smallest of tasks became burdensome. In Rothaynen, the Kingdom of Graedon, the land was ready for a rest from the years of bumper yields of food that fed the people. Pettiness, however, flourished like weeds in an open field. The old stories of chivalry, courtliness and courage were reduced to fantasy and illusion. Courtesy and respect were all but a notion in these sophisticated times. Notwithstanding, the old tales would touch a young heart, and then it was all ready to start once again.

Opportunity was not distributed equally, and those in power pressed their advantage. Still, a young boy with a pure heart and dreams of good will was bent on policing His Majesty's roads and forests. Although the dream was far from his station in life, he wanted so desperately to be a knight. He saw himself as a worthy and noble knight who would intervene on the king's behalf. He would use wisdom in judgment to solve disputes among the people. He would defend the ladies and make war on his king's enemies.

The nobles' children could be assured the right to become knights because not only did they receive the best education available, but they held land and wealth. They learned to read and write, which in itself distinguished them into an elite handful of people. To be born a noble and have land meant that your family certainly knew how to fight and defend it. Every one else had to gain the right in the eyes of God.

The young boy dreamed of hacking his way past a winged serpent or ferocious dragon and definitely rescuing a damsel in distress. Of course, this was the romanticism in him, a far cry from the practical attitudes of the time. The two extremes would clash in him. It was this romanticism, a gift for hope of what should be that would lead him to a life and death crisis of the heart. His name was Brandyn, and he came from the Wendover Lowlands.

The Wendover Lowlands were situated on the western side of the eastern range of the high rocks of the Wendover escarpment. The escarpment stretched for many miles along the coast of the Mare Grigio, a salt sea, and marked the kingdom's southeastern border. On the west side of the escarpment there were rolling hills and fertile soil that stretched for miles in every direction with the odd patch of forest dabbed here and there to provide shade and otherwise a change of scenery. There were numerous small winding creeks of fresh water that found their way to the sea. The region was ideal for growing wheat, oats, barley and other grains. Although every farmer had common livestock such as chickens, pigs, goats or sheep and a cow, and every farmer grew some vegetables to meet their needs, the kingdom looked to the Wendover Lowlands as their primary supply of grains. In Wendover the terrain was ideal for growing grains in great volume.

Almost in the centre of it all, was the small village of Wendover, where people met to sell or trade goods. It was a good place to be if you needed work or needed help. People gathered there whether for business or Sundays to worship at the church. Plenitude Church was the most prominent structure in Wendover. It was hewn of stone quarried from the Wendover escarpment. The interior was decorated with wood works from the thick beam structure and roof, to the rows of church pews and carvings. The thick wood came from the forest east of the Bendire Monastery. The Bendire monks themselves cut down and felled the trees for the purpose.

The building of the church was commissioned by Pastor Mattews, who had been a former knight of Peregren. When he left, he joined the Bendire Monastery that was near King Graedon's castle at Braemar. It was rumored that he had grown weary of battle and was tired of the pettiness at court. Mattews had enough of the illusion of administering justice. A knight that he was friends with, who was younger than he, was ambushed. The death occurred under suspicious circumstances as well. There were those who could affect rulings to their advantage due to their wealth and might. When the mighty were in the right, they won. When the mighty were wrong, they changed the rules or merely took what they wanted anyway. Perhaps that was the explanation for his white hair at so young an age. The fact was, the early white hair was a family trait. The true reason for Mattews turning to the church, he never revealed to anyone.

The Wendover community was overcome with the advent of a former knight whose reputation preceded him. Although he walked away from knighthood and abandoned his lands to a relative, Mattews was loved for his kind deeds. He had been schooled by his mother in the biblical texts. She was a noble woman, and he gained much wisdom from her. He was an excellent speaker who could move the people to the point of action. After his arrival, the building of the church became a priority and developed into a community event. Everyone in Wendover helped out with the building of the church and a modest house for Pastor Mattews. The house was attached to the church by a wall that extended from the church to the dwelling. The two structures were divided by a garden and courtyard. The pastor cherished the garden where he enjoyed working the soil, planting and nurturing plants and flowers to grow. Apart from the smaller craft shops, a farrier and iron worker kept a stable that was important to the Wendover farming community. The other notable building was the Wendover Tavern. Home to spirits and ale, the tavern served as an official meeting place for town meetings to discuss town affairs. The tavern also included a post office for sending or receiving the king's post.

One day while working in the Wendover Tavern, which Brandyn's father and mother, Malcolm and Andrea operated, the king's men came riding through. They were on their way to meet an invading force that was scouted not far from there on the sea coast. When food supplies were short, rather than risk famine, sickness and death, foreigners would raid Wendover, a sure source of food. Foreign warriors often came to raid the Wendover Lowlands, the kingdom's chief source of oats, wheat and barley grains. They would come and take what they wanted by way of food, livestock and any grain that was stored. They also took liberties with the people, young women in general, and would not think twice about killing anyone who opposed them. The invaders also liked to torch dwellings. The sense that the peasant farmers would rebuild their homes and pick up their lives as opposed to organizing and training for combat must have been a reason for this practice. In any event, it was demoralizing to have an invader have his way with your property and then torch it because it was dispensable to them. There were many ships spotted on the sea. With the force they mustered, it looked as though they meant to stay this time.

While the king's men were stationed there, there was need of food and drink for them and also oats and hay for the horses. The party of knights and soldiers were very hungry and very thirsty. They settled in an encampment between Wendover and the sea coast, where the warring raiders would disembark. The king sent his forces to make sure the grain supply was protected and, of course, the people, who did the work too. At harvest time the defending forces came and occupied the area. Since they did not know when the enemy would attack, their presence was as early as mid-August. It lasted until the king's portion of harvested grain shipments could be sent to the granaries in King Graedon's castle at Rothaynen. After that, with a token force, the Wendover Lowlands people were on their own again.

It would have made sense to build and maintain a castle in the area to house the king's forces and to provide this protection for the farmers year round. The presence of a castle would deter the raiders; if not, at least the people would have a place to run to with their families. They would have walls and weapons to defend themselves. Proper granaries could also be built to safely store the grains. The presence of a castle would make more people come to settle the area. More grains could be sown and harvested. The surplus grain could be traded. Such an undertaking required ambition, money, labour and, foremost, time. Although it was a good idea to build a castle and then populate the region, there was also the idea that a navy should be built. A navy could be used for trade as well as defence. Neither plan was economically viable for the time being.

The last major construction of a castle in Rothaynen was the king's new castle. Graedon's father, King Orendyn, had decided to build a new castle on Thermanden Bay. The new castle that he named Braemar was more central, had a greater volume of water around it and could better extend Rothaynen's influence eastward toward Mead and Wendover. Orendyn's previous castle at Peregren had also been very strategic because the mountains behind it were a source of iron for making weapons. To its immediate north and east, there was timber, which was thought could never be exhausted. When Peregren castle was built, its sole priority was defence. Its back was nestled against a mountain wall that stretched out like a corridor. Of course, the all-important garden food stuffs were grown on the other side of that mountain corridor at Marmora. Marmora was bordered by the mountains at its back and the River Brae to its south. Although it was the finest, rich, black soil, farmland in

Marmora was limited. In some places the land was overworked. If the kingdom was to expand, they would need a reliable source of grains. The lowlands of Wendover, with the many streams running through, was the prize where grains could be sown as far as the eye could see. The golden harvest was truly worth its weight in gold.

In an effort to expand Rothaynen's influence over Wendover grains, the Dolometen Arms Tower was built as a token of commitment to the well-being of the farmers. It was located on the coast of the Wendover escarpment. In a previous raid, the castle was sacked and burned. The stone ruin is all that remains. In actuality, it was more of a watch tower with a small hall than a castle. Although it was situated strategically, that is you could effectively observe all seafaring vessels if there was no fog, you could not tell friend from foe until the ships were upon you. It was difficult to determine whether the ships in the harbour were fishing vessels landing for supplies and trade of their goods or enemy vessels. Sometimes the villagers and traders quarrelled in an effort to strike the best bargain. Even trading is not as easy as it sounds, so the king's soldiers had to police the trading as well.

It was not even a foggy day when the Dolometen Arms Tower was attacked. The watchmen were not alerted until the enemy was disembarking from the war vessel. The watchtower was not even the target. It was an early summer raid. The pirates from the islands of Orgol, at the far east end of the Aggregian Sea, had run short of food while returning to their homeland. They decided to test the resolve of the Wendover farmers. The Orgol plunderers had slipped into the nearest farms and collected what they could by means of food supplies and were on their way back to their boat. It was too late to chase after them at the farms. In response, the small garrison of the king's men, who were summoned from the tavern, responded by attacking the few raiders left behind to guard their landing boats. The king's men were routing the raiders. Upon the return of the raiding parties, however, the kings' men realized that they were outnumbered and decided to retreat to the tower. Confident of success, the Orgols sent the stolen supplies to their ship. Angered by the assault on their landing boats, the Orgols decided to attack the retreating soldiers. They sent their landing boats to load their ship and then return toward the shore before the tower. In the meantime, the landed party of Orgols set out to pursue the guards who had retreated to the safety of the tower. The Orgol looters surrounded the tower and set fire to the thick wooden doors. They exchanged arrows through the narrow windows. In due time though, the fire and smoke drew out the men into open battle. Outnumbered and drunk, the king's men were all killed by the raiders. The Orgols then set fire to the hall. They then returned to their landing boats and rowed for their ship that would sail them away.

So here were the king's men come again to make preparations to protect the people and grains. During the meal that was prepared for them, a few soldiers got boisterous and made passes at the tavern keeper's daughter Meaghan. Meaghan was a tall, slim girl with a fair complexion and long hazel hair. Malcolm, the girl's father, thought it better to weather the insult since it was in the presence of many soldiers and drink had taken a part. When Brandyn noticed what was going on, he did not dismiss the insult so quickly. He immediately sprang to Meaghan's rescue and stood between his sister and the soldier. The soldier, better for the ale he consumed, took his knife and slashed at Brandyn with a deliberate lunge. While he distracted the rogue, he noted that Meaghan ran to her mother Andrea in the kitchen. With Meaghan safely away, Brandyn gracefully moved out of harm's way. The drunken soldier stumbled to the ground with his weapon.

Great laughter ensued over the incident. The soldier became infuriated. The soldier's friend noticed what a fool his partner was made to look. He extended his leg out to trip Brandon so he could be taught a lesson. When Brandyn tripped back, the drunken soldier grabbed the youth. His intentions were to hurt him. He held his knife up against the boy's throat.

"Perhaps a memento of this night would teach you a lesson, boy," the soldier ground while clenching his teeth. He would have surely sliced away at the youth's face carelessly. In the commotion, Brandyn's father and mother were appealing for the man not to harm their son. They too were caught up in the crowd and were barred from approaching by the crowd of soldiers. The consensus was that this youth had shown no respect and insulted one of their own. In all that had ensued, a knife managed to slip by all gathered there and was placed against the drunken soldier's throat.

The cloaked man who spoke with a firm voice calmly said, "Let the boy go."

The rogue paused, relented and then released his hostage. At the other end of the tavern entered Lord Barton. He commanded the assembly of the king's men and returned from inspecting the soldiers' encampment. Upon word from him, his escort of soldiers arrested and removed the drunken soldier from the tavern.

There was a silence while the man removed his cloak and revealed his face. It was a well-respected knight who returned from his surveying. His name was Woodcroft of Galles from the far west. He looked around at the men who listened with intent as he spoke.

"We are not the invaders!" said the knight with conviction. "We were summoned to protect these good people from them. Remember!"

After a pause, Lord Barton reiterated, "Remember yourselves! Save your fight for the enemy. Get rest for the matter and tasks ahead. Go on!"

A few things were said under the soldiers' breaths but everyone began to leave. With everyone leaving, it seemed that the episode was over.

Malcolm was grateful for this youthful and wise knight's actions. He was the son of Welledon, the Duke of Galles. Who knows what might have happened had he not intervened?

"I thank you for what you did. I have always heard good things about Welledon and, now, his son."

"What happened was regretful. We are truly sorry," was his sincere reply.

In the meantime, Meaghan and her mother were spying into the tavern from the back room. Lord Barton approached the tavern owner with a little sack of gold pieces for payment. He handed them to Malcolm. "We are ever grateful for your hospitality." He paused. "My apologies for the incident. It has been dealt with."

"The king's men have always been welcome in our parts," replied Malcolm.

So the tavern was nearly empty as Lord Barton left. Woodcroft had been out scouting their defences and arrived late, but apparently just in time to save Brandyn. He had not eaten and had hoped to secure a meal before retiring for the night.

"You probably haven't eaten as yet," noted the tavern keeper.

Malcolm summoned Andrea and Meaghan to bring bread and ale for this brave knight. Andrea brought the knight some ale, but he politely requested water instead. Meaghan brought him bread and some butter made from fresh milk earlier that day. She caught his eye. Her face and hair and hands: it was hard to resist looking at the young lady. Meaghan found herself attracted to him as well.

In the meantime, Malcolm stood assessing in his mind. His son may have been injured badly or even killed, and what about his daughter?

In these times, many a young, innocent maiden had been taken advantage of without any recourse of action against the perpetrator. It was a villain's world. Right or wrong, if you wanted something and you took it, all you need to do is fight and win to keep it. So much for honour, dignity, laws and justice. In this day and age, the weak feared and were made to serve the strong: it became a tradition. Ironically, courtliness was the first order of a knight's expectations. Courtliness was simply the manner in which people were to be treated without regard to their wealth or strength. A gentleman's expectation was no less. For a society to be civilized, the treatment of men, women, children, those who could not fend for themselves and everyone, for that matter, would have to be fair and just.

Brandyn went over to the knight with the intention of thanking him, but he did not know how to start.

The knight said to him," You might have been hurt."

Brandon wasted no time complaining. "He should not have bothered my sister. A soldier in the service of the king should protect the king's subjects. They even rose up against my parents, who have done nothing but support them."

"Sometimes it is very hard to distinguish who the enemy is. We are imposing on you in somewhat the same manner as the king's enemies. The difference should be that we employ manners, respect your dignity and guard your rights."

"That soldier was hardly a gentleman, and would never make a good knight," lit the youth.

"What do you know about knighthood?"

"I know a knight is to show courtliness toward a lady and chivalry in the face of adversity. He is to uphold truth, honour and be generous." He paused. "I know that a knight would not be the cause of trouble for a young lady."

"You certainly showed chivalry when you came to your sister's aid. By the way, my name is Woodcroft."

"Brandyn."

The knight was most impressed with this youth's manner; the enthusiasm was inspiring. He took a closer look at Brandyn. His physical stature was impressive for his age. He was tall and slim, clean favoured with long light brown hair. Woodcroft was so impressed with Brandyn's enthusiasm that he did not even consult his parents before proposing an idea. Woodcroft spontaneously said, "Well, Brandyn, my squire recently had an untimely death with a sickness of the lungs, and I have not as yet found a worthy squire. Tell me, would your parents object to serving His Majesty by becoming my squire?"

It was Welledon's son who was asking. This opportunity fell to nobles and their children. It was an offer that every boy dreamed of. Malcolm could not believe his ears. He could not object to the offer made by Woodcroft. Although Andrea had her reservations, she did not speak them in the presence of this esteemed knight. Andrea was altogether against it; Brandyn was her only son. She did not need him gallivanting around with tin men to be slain on some battlefield far from home. Woodcroft's good name, sincerity and reputation preceded him. Although Brandyn was needed on the farm, this was an opportunity not every boy got. Malcolm literally had no choice. Usually the children that came from a wealthy family served as pages in the castle court with other wealthy children. From there, as they grew older, a sponsoring knight, usually a relative or by other arrangement, would make them their squire. This was Welledon's heir that wanted Brandyn to be his squire. How could they deny their son the opportunity of being a squire for Woodcroft?

So Brandyn became Woodcroft's squire and served him and Vento, Woodcroft's steed, quite capably.

Challenges

Meanwhile in Huynste, King Nodunn had finalized his plans. Huynste referred to the lands of a sea faring people who lived on a group of islands and some rocky mainland in the East Aggregian Sea. The mainland they inhabited served as the crucial hub of a trade route. The Huynsten people, by virtue of conquering the mainland across from their islands, controlled that trade route. The Huynsten ships traditionally raided and plundered for the goods they needed to survive. Due to their control of the trade route, the caravans and merchants came naturally to their crossroads to do business. Some traders tried to avoid the traditional trade route and ship by sea, but they risked being raided by pirates. The Huynsten merchants at Tirmiz, the city of trade, were not fair traders and then there was their king's tax. Nodunn the Huynsten king was angered with his loss of revenue from Tirmiz. Nodunn encouraged his ships to raid all sea commerce at will. At the height of his power, he sent out a land army to spread his influence further into the Great Continent. Since Nodunn's councillors had advised him to secure a region where a source of grain was available, the answer was the Wendover Lowlands. He sent a large fleet of ships to invade there too. It was not a good idea to divide and spread his forces so thinly, but this was King Nodunn, who had never tasted defeat.

Nodunn had amassed for himself, from other cultures that he conquered, an invading force to take and occupy the Wendover

Lowlands forever. The meeting in his temple on the island of Merkor gathered all the smaller kings so he could set before them the task at hand. Nodunn proclaimed, "Each of you kings will rule the land that you conquer. We will set up trade amongst ourselves and sell our surplus on our terms. And for these rights, you will pay me a tribute annually."

Nodunn had struck an accord with all his kings. He himself was, of course, to be the king of kings. So his forces set out for Wendover in great numbers.

Brandyn's first serious action came in repelling the invasion that did come to Wendover by the Huynstens. The Huynstens were serious about invading this time. It seemed as though they sent all their warships. Their sails with the black octopus were spotted by fisherman in the Mare Grigio en route to Wendover. Their armies would outnumber King Graedon's forces at Wendover by four to one. A messenger was sent from Wendover to Braemar Castle to inform Graedon he would need to send more men and supplies, but at this point it was too late. Graedon himself was absent due to his health. The army was entrusted to Lord Barton, his cousin. There was some good fortune for the people of Wendover though. It happened that three warships from Craigroyston were also in the south Mare Grigio area. With the help of these ships from Craigroyston, a united kingdom to the north, the Huynsten ships could be engaged in a naval battle as well. If the naval battle slowed down the landing of their forces, it could just give Graedon's forces a chance to face their enemy in smaller waves. There was no way to communicate this message and no guarantee that the three Craigroyston ships would engage a navy with larger numbers.

Huysten ships were not popular in Craigroyston. They constantly raided fishing vessels from Craigroyston that were exporting cod stocks or wool south to Leems for trade. Huynsten ships that were based in the East Aggregian Sea raided all sea faring commerce at will. The navy of Craigroyston was developed for the purpose of guarding their ships from pirates. On that day, the three warships from Craigroyston were sailing down the eastern coast on their way to meet and escort commerce coming from Leems. They spotted the large armada of Huynsten ships on the Mare Grigio. After monitoring their movements on the high seas, there was no question in their captain's mind that the Huynsten ships were headed for the harbour at Wendover.

The number of Huynsten ships was much greater than the three ships from Craigroyston's fleet. However, Selwyck, the captain of the ships from Craigroyston, was under orders from King Jonquis to engage and sink Huynsten warships. On this occasion it seemed that those orders amounted to a suicide mission for the Craigroyston ships. Nevertheless, the *Bravada*, *Courage* and *Victory* would do their duty as best they could. Selwyck noted that the Huynsten ships that were close to the harbour had already begun to discharge the smaller boats to land their equipment and forces. Selwyck's decision to engage the Huynsten navy had nothing to do directly with saving Wendover. Selwyck saw an opportunity to hurt his people's enemy. Afterall, Graedon's forces could easily mistake them for the enemy as well. The mutual dislike for the aggressive Huynsten's carried the day and allied Craigroyston to Rothaynen for the battle.

For the first time the presence of a navy friendly to Wendover gave the Huynsten invaders something to worry about, as their means of landing on shore and escape to the sea was threatened. In the Wendover plains the Huynstens could not land their entire force of warriors as planned. The ships at the back had to wait for the ships in the harbour to finish sending in their men. There was confusion as more men were engaged to defend on the Huynsten ships in the harbour. The Huynsten warriors were concerned about the safety of their ships, their ability to be supplied on land and their retreat. It seemed that the Huynsten's surprise invasion provided them with a surprise as well.

The screeching sound of fireballs launched from the enemy ships catapults could be heard from the harbour. It was not long before they made their way on the beaches of Wendover's harbour. The fireballs were large rounded stones that were robed in sack cloth and soaked in linseed oil. When they came crashing toward a field army or enemy ship, disaster would ensue. Selwyck knew that if he engaged the Huynsten warships in battle, he could not outlast their fire power. There were too many of them. Selwyck was severely outnumbered. Huynsten ships that were far back on the open sea took note of Craigroyston's flag and opened fire on the three ships. Selwyck neither ran off nor did he respond by returning fire. He believed that at that distance, the lack of accuracy would be a waste of ammunition. Selwyck looked at the Wendover harbour and realized that while the small boats were ferrying Huynsten's invading force, these warships were sitting ducks. If Selwyck sailed his ships into the harbour, the Huynsten ships that were afar would have to stop firing at them or risk hitting their own ships. With this manoeuvre he would create anxiety and confusion. Selwyck could effectively keep the ships that were afar out of the battle while he faced the vulnerable ships in the harbour.

Selwyck gave word by flag that his ships should sail straight for the Wendover harbour. As anticipated, there was some hesitation from the *Courage* and *Victory*, but when they saw the *Bravada* sail straight for the Wendover harbour, they followed. The Huynsten ships at the back stopped firing on them as they entered the harbour. However, the enemy ships in the harbour were in close range and, despite the limited manpower, began to fire upon them. Selwyck concentrated the attack on the ships in the harbour that had discharged their landing boats. They were anchored and could not move. There was a sense of surprise that the three ships from Craigroyston would attack at all. Although he knew he was outnumbered, he realized that his naval command would never have this excellent opportunity to inflict heavy losses on their enemy's navy again.

In the exchange of fire, the *Victory* sailed into the Huynsten ships that were turned broadside. *Victory* managed to sail alongside a

Huynsten ship with its oars in the water. The weight of the ship and its speed snapped the oars in two, rendering them useless. Some of the fireballs launched by the Huynsten ships flew right across the bow of *Bravada* and landed on their own ships. The Huynsten crews men were taken by surprise and in the panic that ensued, accidents were made. Nevertheless, the Huynsten warriors rallied to their cause and adjusted their fire. The hail of arrows that the two navies exchanged looked like a swarm of locusts.

The Huynsten ships from afar had stopped their firing. They were concerned about hitting one of their own ships. They could do nothing but wait and watch. The Huynsten ships in the harbour opened their deadly accurate fire at point blank range. The Craigroyston ships were very effective too as they swiftly sailed in a close range. In effect, Selwyck let fly with his archers arrows set aflame. These too were fired at close deadly range. The crossfire wreaked havoc on both warring sides, and the smell of burning oil, wood, sail tarp and blood filled the air.

On the lowlands, Lord Barton and Woodcroft had positioned King Graedon's forces on the higher ground facing the enemy. The archers were positioned behind the front lines at the proper distance to fire their arrows. If the archers could inflict some losses early, that would make a magnificent psychological advantage. A dead warrior compelled his comrades to fight on and avenge, but a wounded warrior who was not dead reminded everyone of the pain and gore that accompanied battle. The wounded needed tending and would want to retreat.

The Huynsten warships that were turned on their broadside launched a barrage of arrows and fireballs that rolled on the land. The early balls of fire got trapped on the beach against the sand bluffs. As the Huynsten artillery crews adjusted their trajectory, the fireballs cleared the beach and sent portions of Graedon's front line soldiers reeling to get out of the path.

With the noise of the commotion back in the harbour, the Huynsten invaders rowing toward the beach looked back with concern. They followed through with their orders to land and form attack groups, however, they kept looking back. The Huynstens did not break ranks and kept their formations as more and more landed. Their large shields took the brunt of arrows from Wendover's defenders. The Huynsten lines were steadfast though. They began to advance like a unit. The pounding drums and battle cries kept them focused. Huynsten archers kept busy by letting fly their arrows. Onward they marched, in full armour and with all manner of weapons that they could carry.

The balls of fire hurled by the Huynsten warships on the coastal strip all but stopped. Fewer and fewer fireballs were launched. The Huynsten ships in the harbour were now engaged with firing at the Craigroyston ships. The firing was at a close and deadly range. The distraction was of great benefit to the Wendover defenders. The flow of men off the Huynsten ships had effectively been stopped as the ships had to defend against the sea attack. Lord Barton instructed his archers to continue to let fly their arrows, but the landed foe kept advancing. It was at this point that Woodcroft suggested to Lord Barton that a full out charge might be in order since the enemy had been isolated. There were no new landing boats launched to bring reinforcements or supplies. Their archers were running low on arrows. Lord Barton agreed with that notion and was waiting for the right moment.

Lord Barton gave word to the knights to ready their sections for an all-out advance on his order. On such a wide front, it would take some time to communicate the command. As they waited, the Huynsten army kept their arrows flying, thus depleting their supply. Not every section of the Wendover forces had been contacted when a great explosion took place in the harbor. There was smoke in the harbor. The Huynsten ships from afar could not tell what was going on. Graedon's forces could see that a few Huynsten ships had caught fire. The ships from Craigroyston bore their share of fire damage too. Then the moment that Lord Barton had waited for came. Another Huynsten warship exploded when fire caught a store of linseed oil on the ship. The tall mast snapped as the fire consumed it and it fell onto the ship's deck. The Huynsten banner crashed into the water. The accident split the ship in two, and there was turmoil on its deck. It gave the Huynsten land force something to think about. That was the moment that Lord Barton had waited for.

"Archers! Fire three more waves of arrows! Lancers! Prepare to advance!" Lord Barton paused and then he yelled, "Chaaarrrggge!!!"

All the knights bolstered their men. The foot soldiers with their swords drawn and spears men all advanced in a fury. The archers fired their three waves of arrows in rapid succession in order to precede the arrival of the charging men. Graedon's knights, who would usually engage enemy knights, had no adversary. There were no Huynsten knights or horses on the beach to fight with. In place of a lance, they drew their swords. Some called to their squires to fetch an axe or mace. It was Brandyn's first battle as a squire. Given the size of the enemy force, it was baptism by fire for him. Although he was afraid, Brandyn stayed alert and followed the other squires lead in assisting their lords. The entire encampment rode, ran or marched to battle. From the "a cavallo" position, the knights swept in and cut down the enemy ground force. The foot soldiers then advanced against an army in utter turmoil. When the two armies clashed, the fighting on the beach was fierce "mano a mano" combat. The blood ran off the beach and flowed into the sea. Back in camp, the squires could smell the blood in the damp air as well.

In the midst of the successful crossfire to this point, Lieutenant Jonas of the *Bravada* recommended that they cross back over to the north side and fly on the high seas. The damage to their ships was not grave. They could still make it home. Instead, Selwyck issued the command to keep firing until all their munition supplies were exhausted. "I want our ships to be so light that they can race back home on a breeze," he inspired. Selwyck also commanded that his ships continue to cross sail and weave back and forth in the harbour through the Huynsten armada. After all, the Huynsten ships at the back were out of the fight. They dared not fire while their own ships were in such close proximity.

Selwyck had divided the large Huynsten navy into a sector that he could deal with. The naval battle now depended on the quickness and accuracy of the ballistae crews. The Huynsten's already lost two ships in the harbour and a few others were battered and burning severely. Most of their crews were engaged controlling the fires. The damage to Selwyck's ship, the *Bravada*, was extensive as was the *Courage*. There were dead mariners lying on the deck from the arrows having pierced them. There were fewer and fewer men to fight the fires. The *Victory* was bludgeoned with flaming arrows and fireballs, burned and sank. Fortunately, the surviving boat men swam onto the escarpment's long beach.

The Huynsten ships could have fought on and finished off the Craigroyston warships. They could have continued with their plan and landed the rest of their invasion force. In the surprise and confusion, however, the battered Huynstens on the battlefield were in retreat. They were anxious to row out to any ship that would take them away from there. The command ship, somewhere in the centre of the armada, had no way of knowing the number of Graedon's forces on the land. All they knew was that there was smoke and fire coming from the battlefield and their first wave had failed. At seeing the Huynsten warriors retreat to their landing boats, the rest of the armada chose to return to the safety of the high seas. It was unclear whether they might attack again or sail back to their islands.

Selwyck was forced to land at Wendover to request permission to make necessary repairs to his ships. There he collected the survivors of the *Victory* who swam ashore to the beach before the Wendover escarpment. The wounded Huynsten warriors, that were all that was left of the original force, were allowed to return to their landing boats and row for their ships. There were numerous landing boats left behind. Lord Barton was ever grateful for the heroic antics of this young sea captain from Craigroyston. Graedon had sent Barton and Woodcroft to reinforce the army he sent to Wendover from Braemar. Even then, their forces would not have been enough. Despite the steadfast Woodcroft and his forces from Galles, and

Barton's force from Teresforte, it would not have been enough. Wendover, its people, resources and land would have been lost that very day. With the Huynstens firmly established in Wendover, it would be a matter of time before they attacked further inland at Braemar Castle before winter set in. Barton realized that Graedon's forces could not have won the day if it were not for the intervention of Selwyck and his ships. It was bravery extraordinary. Upon making his introduction to Selwyck, Lord Barton remarked, "They should have named you 'Bravada'."

Repairs to the ships were made hastily in anticipation of the Huynstens redoubling their efforts. Woodcroft sent scouts up and down the Wendover coast in the event that the Huynsten ships tried to land their forces there. Lord Barton had requisitioned more supplies and waited intently for them. He ordered Selwyck's two ships to be rearmed the moment that the supplies arrived. The threat of another attack was imminent. Lieutenant Jonas wondered what they were expected to do with two battered ships against an armada. He pressed Selwyck to leave. Selwyck decided to stay. Federics and his force from Peregren arrived to reinforce and resupply the Wendover forces. Graedon had summoned Federics to reinforce Wendover even before he received Barton's dispatch. In the meantime, there was an effort to collect and bury the fallen soldiers from both armies. The burying of fallen soldiers was important for health reasons. Vultures and other birds of prey were trying to feast on the dead carcasses. The dead Huynsten warriors were piled on the beach and burned. The caves in the escarpment were close at hand for the burial of Graedon's fallen men. Pastor Mattews was on hand to administer final rites. They had to work swiftly, as there was a risk that a plague could spread. If that happened, the victory would go to their enemy. The anticipated renewed Huynsten offensive did not come.

At Wendover, a great feast to feed the brave men who fought was organized. Lord Barton sent word to King Graedon about the support that Craigroyston's navy gave against the Huynstens. Lord Barton suggested that an emissary be sent to thank King Jonquis. King Graedon would go further and invite King Jonquis and Queen Enyja to Rothaynen for the Harvest Moonfest Games that would take place in the month. With the blessings and help of the people of Wendover, Selwyck was able to take on repairs, food supplies and stones quarried from the Wendover escarpment without delay.

While taking on the repairs, it was determined that the *Bravada* was damaged too badly. The rib structure of the ship was damaged and there was no way to make a new rib. The farmers of Wendover did not have the tools or skills it took to make ribs for a large ship or the proper wood. On the rocking high seas the wave-tossed vessel would take on water and surely sink. Selwyck could not abandon the vessel at Wendover since there was no formal treaty between the two countries. The damaged ship could easily be used as a model for the building of a navy. So Selwyck came up with a diplomatic solution. In keeping with the funeral rites of Craigton, the fallen mariners of the Craigroyston ships were recovered. The honourable dead mariners were washed and sewn into linen sheet covers. They were then placed on the *Bravada* that would provide their transport to Heaven.

Pastor Mattews was on hand to assist with the burial rites. The *Bravada* was sailed away toward the high seas. *Courage*, the only remaining Craigroyston ship, escorted the vessel out to collect the sailors who guided her away. After reaching deep waters in the Mare Grigio, the sailors that ferried *Bravada* and Pastor Mattews, who delivered final rites, boarded the *Courage*. A final prayer was offered by Pastor Mattews.

"The Lord is my Shepherd, there is nothing I shall want. Fresh and green are the pastures where He gives me repose. Near restful waters He leads me to revive my drooping spirit.

"Yea though I walk in the valley of the shadow of the dead, none ill shall I fear. You are with me and Your rod and staff. With these You bring comfort.

"You prepare a banquet for me in the sight of my enemies. My head You anoint with oil. My cup, it runs over.

"Surely goodness and kindness shall follow me all the days of my life. In the Lord's own home will I dwell forever and ever. Amen."

The drummers, dressed in ceremonial robes, drummed a slow, solemn funeral march. As tradition dictated, five archers in full armor with scarlet robes and head gear, lit their arrowheads with fire. At the conclusion of the prayer, in unison the archers took aim, drew back their bows and let their arrows fly toward the deck of the *Bravada.* The arrows found their mark. The linseed oil that was poured over the ship's deck caught fire. There was a silence as they all watched from the deck of the *Courage.* The trumpets then belted out a crisp farewell. As the flame grew and crackling could be heard, Selwyck lost focus of the world around him. As he looked at the burning ship, he was able to see, hear, and feel the agony and sorrow and strife that went with the struggle to oppose evil. Upright men had no choice: to allow evil to flourish was to ask for even more suffering. Selwyck's men had fought bravely but as he looked, it seemed as if the battle continued. He saw battle scenes in the fire that replayed themselves from his memory. There were even scenes from the battle on land. Then, rising from the flames, he saw his men and others ascending upward. One of his mariners looked back at him expressionless while the others urged him on. Selwyck said nothing of this to the others around him. What did this man want to tell him?

Pastor Mattews concluded with a prayer for the present crew to have a safe, swift journey home. Then he disembarked the ship for a small boat with Barton and Woodcroft, who were on board to observe the ceremony and pay respect. Although the ship was out quite a distance, there were many observers on the coast that climbed the Wendover escarpment to get a good look at the ship set afire. It was not their custom to cremate their dead. They did not see or hear or feel what Selwyck did. Selwyck even saw some men stop their fight and reach up for help but they sank with the burning ship.They watched in silence until the ship perished into the depths of the sea, never to return. With that the vision ended too.

We Will Never Be Slaves

Despite the accolades that Selwyck received for his courageous decision to enter the battle at the Wendover harbour, there were those who thought differently. Lieutenant Jonas had suggested leaving after one crisscross of the Huynsten ships in the Wendover harbour. If he had his way, he would have left the battle after the minimum engagement. This plan, he reasoned, would have assisted their neighbours and assured their safe escape. If he was in charge, Jonas would not have continued the engagement in the Wendover harbour against the Huynsten armada. That was his plan.

Jonas came from a long line of navy men at Craigton. Selwyck did not. He was bitter that two of their ships now lay at the bottom of the Mare Grigio and with them, noble mariners. These feelings were acknowledged by every mariner of the Craigroyston ships, but not all would blame Selwyck. Most believed that they had done their duty. If they had run after limited engagement, the Huynstens would be in Wendover this very moment. Jonas, however, would make a full report upon their return to Craigroyston. Jonas would cite that although it was their duty to protect their commerce on the high seas, the Huynstens were attacking a foreign harbour. Two ships and seaworthy mariners were lost. After the burial on the third day at Wendover, Selwyck decided it was time to be on his way home with what was left of his sailors.

It was Jonas' right to report the matter of the battle at the Wendover harbour to the commander of the navy. Arturus, the commander of the navy, received Jonas' report. He also received Selwyck for a debriefing before they went to the Karley, which was the name for the royal court. Jonquis and Enyja were anxious to hear about the event from their own naval captain. An envoy of King Graedon's court was dispatched the moment he learned of the battle. The envoy had travelled by land and arrived before Selwyck with the news. Graedon's emissary conveyed a "thank you" for the bravery of the Craigroyston naval ships and their Captain Selwyck. Selwyck's act, though under orders, committed Craigroyston to be at war with the Huynstens. Some councillors wanted to blame Selwyck for inciting the Huynstens. Nobody likes to be at war. The fact was, they were already at war with the Huynstens anyway.

The facts would come out at court and the truth would be known. The Karley heard the testimony of the many mariners who gave brave accounts of their resolve. The Karley heard Lieutenant Jonas and Captain Selwyck too. There was great deliberation within the court and the galleries that overlooked it. Accusations of glory seeking and madness reared their ugly heads. In the commotion that nearly ensued, when mothers, widows and orphans of the deceased sailors were informed of their loss, it was Queen Enyja that brought order to the affair. After silencing the assembly, Enyja posed Selwyck a single question. "Why did you engage the Huynsten fleet, Captain Selwyck?"

"Your Majesty must know of the navy's loyalty to Craigroyston. With a destructive force of that size and the Huynstens' reckless demeanour, there was no doubt that they had intentions to invade our neighbours. They would have been successful at annihilating all of King Graedon's forces. Once established in Wendover, they would attack and lay siege on the king's castle at Braemar before winter."

"What does that have to do with us?" interrupted a councillor.

CAYUGA SECONDARY SCHOOL
LIBRARY

"With all due respect,"responded Jonquis, "We have heard from everyone without prejudice, and we wish to hear from our naval captain. We will give him the respect and courtesy that we all deserve."

"Thank you, Your Majesty." Selwyck paused. "If Wendover fell to the Huynstens, they would gain the resources there. The grains could satisfy their need for food. The people there would be forced into servitude while their army laid siege to Braemar. With a weakened army, Braemar would eventually fall. If Braemar was lucky to survive the winter, then Huynsten ships could sail across the River Brae, avoiding the mighty caste at Teresforte. They could merely sail into the heart of the country. Eventually Braemar Castle would fall. As Braemar fell to siege, Peregren would be next. Peregren is where armaments are made in their iron works, so the Huynstens could rearm themselves without having to be supplied from their homeland. To the north of Peregren lies Roysford and our southern gate. They could literally march through the pasture lands of Roysford. From the sea they could put a naval blockade around Norsendan in the north sea and attack Craigton."

"What about their legendary Petrinvincit?" yelled a councillor.

"Do you know how many ships it would take to bottle up Norsendan?" yelled out an observer in the gallery.

"We will tolerate no more interruptions," declared Queen Enyja. "You may continue, Captain."

"In answer to the questions put forth, Petrinvincit, the castle at Teresforte, could literally be ignored. After the rest of Rothaynen fell, Petrinvincit would be alone. Eventually it would have to surrender. As for the number of ships it would take to block Norsendan, we got to see what that looks like. In the end we would have to face our enemy at our harbor and on our own homeland. We would be hemmed in. We would need to commit every man, woman and child to combat for our very existence."

"If Your Majesty will permit, I have a question for our captain," appealed a councillor named Evan. With a nod of approval from

Jonquis he continued, "There has been testimony from everyone that the Huynsten force was large. If they were so large, why did they leave? How do we know that the Huynsten invasion, if it was an invasion, would have been successful that day?"

"Councillor, the Huynsten ships retreated because of the bravery of our mariners who stood up to tyranny. Graedon's force on the beaches were dauntless as well. You have my word of honour on it, the testimony of Lieutenant Jonas and all my mariners. The ships sent to Wendover were more than a raiding party. I too was in the midst of the naval battle. Like my boatmen and Jonas, I too could have perished, but all of us did our duty." Selwyck turned toward his monarchs and stressed, "Your Majesties, we would never have the opportunity to do what we did against the Huynstens again."

A cry from the galleries interrupted, "Madness!"

Soon the entire gallery joined in the ruckus. When the noise ceased, Selwyck turned to the Queen. "Your Majesty, we swore an oath to keep the seas safe and ensure that the vital wool, cod and grain trade that is critical to our kingdom's survival would continue undisturbed. It is in thinking of the men, women and children of our country that we engaged the Huynsten threat at that place on that day. We engaged them away from home, and of that I am grateful. The mariners that died in the battle did not do so in vain but as proud subjects of our kingdom. They knew the price. They were selfless warriors. As for the loss of the ships, they can be replaced, and must be replaced with urgency. The men we lost were in my care, under my command, and I have never abused my men or my command. We stood together in defence of our way of life." He paused and then concluded, "We let the Huynsten aggressor, who understand might and only might, know that we would not lay back and wait for our appropriation. Waiting in fear for when they decide that they want what we have worked and sacrificed for. Your Majesties, honourable councillors and good people of Craigroyston, we let them know that we will never be slaves!"

The galleries were silenced and there was a look of pride that came from Jonquis and Enyja. Lieutenant Jonas realized he had misjudged Selwyck, he was every inch a naval captain. He arose from his place and offered his hand to Selwyck. Selwyck took his hand in friendship and Jonas stepped back and saluted him. "My captain!" he exclaimed.

A sense of pride was felt by everyone in the Karley and in the gallery. Despite their sorrow, even the widows and orphans shared the sense of pride that their sacrifice had purpose. It was obvious that Craigroyston was now a growing concern on the high seas and a force to be reckoned with.

A Royal Romance

Craigroyston was made up of two dukedoms that were united by the marriage of their duke's children. The northeast coast dukedom of Craigton was namely home to a fishing and seafaring people. The cliffs and rocks in the area provided good defence against enemies, but the terrain was poor for growing any significant kind of crop. South and west of there, more inland, was Roysford. There were patches of soil for some farming and mainly grazing of sheep for the fabric known as wool. The wool fabric was the best for making clothing that touched human skin. Wool especially came in handy during the colder months from autumn to spring. The demand for wool and the skill to weave it were in great demand. The two dukedoms traded and assisted each other in finding markets and shipping wool clothing to wherever Craigton ships could sell or trade. The vegetables in Roysford were traded with Craigton in exchange for cod stocks that would sustain the people over the winter.

Duke Betrand had a daughter, Ellen, his first born who was betrothed to Prince Mattic of Leems. Leems was their trading partner across the sea on Tamerana, the great continent. Betrand's son, Jonquis, had traveled inland with his father to meet with his neighbor Duke Cardem, who had a lovely daughter Enyja. The business of the court was of no consequence to the young Jonquis and Enyja, who were about twelve and nine years of age. The two managed to slip away from their guardians and travelled to the countryside. They had some adventure that day. Namely, they boasted about their skills. Their walk took them across the meadow. The sun in the sky made it very warm that day so they took cover under the shady forest trees. The path led them by the mountain wall and they decided to climb it. It was during the rock climbing that they were confronted by a fox. A healthy animal would have avoided the encounter, but this fox was rabid.

Although afraid, the both of them, they stood their ground and kept the animal at bay. The fox showed its teeth and growled as its saliva ran out of its mouth. Jonquis had his knife drawn. Enyja was especially accurate at throwing stones. She often competed with her tutor by throwing stones across the castle gardens. Jonquis was frightened and could have run to safety, but he did not want Enyja to think he could not defend her. Instead, Jonquis challenged the animal by taking a swipe at the fox with his knife. The fox was so quick that it dodged the knife's path and repositioned its head to bite the arm of Jonquis just above the hand. That did not deter him from standing his ground bravely. Their guardians and a party of servants who had noted their absence began to search for them. They had found them, and just in time. The fox was sick as it pressed to attack the search party. A healthy animal would have run to safety. Since the fox was outnumbered and distracted, one of the servants hurled a large stone that broke its hind leg. The fox was easily killed after that and had to be buried.

Unfortunately, the fox's bite made Jonquis very sick. Cardem was alarmed that his guest's son was seriously hurt. He called for his physician. He also dispatched a trusted servant, Yonny, to fetch the special horn of Chancery. He was to ride with haste to the west road where it meets the forest gate. At the forest gate Yonny was to blow the horn of Chancery in order to summon the alchemist who lived deep in the forest. The horn was indeed special. As he was told, the horn would not make a sound in the immediate area, but he was to trust that the sound it made would carry for a great distance. Yonny was to blow the horn in succession and listen until he heard a reply. He did as he was told, but he heard no sound as he blew in the horn of Chancery. After what seemed to be an hour, Yonny heard a reply. The servant blew the horn three times in succession and a reply came back three times in succession. At that point, Yonny was sure that the alchemist heard the horn and got the message to come. Yonny blew into the horn one last time and held it as long as he could. He was answered by the same long blast. Yonny returned to Cardem and told him what he had done.

At the castle, Jonquis' wound was bathed by the physician. As time passed, the doctor could not improve the patient's condition. The young prince was given water in an effort to restore fluids and dilute the poison in his body. Cardem was not easy on Enyja. All she could do was look at Jonquis. Betrand was deeply worried as this was his only son. Cardem assured him that the old alchemist would know what to do.

You could see that Enyja was very concerned about this boy. They got along wonderfully as they innocently boasted of their accomplishments. She relived in her mind the entire day that they spent walking through the bedewed grass with the warm sun on their faces. There was a cool forest breeze and the water they drank from the stream was fresh. These thoughts comforted her until she realized that is was now the present. Would Jonquis be alright?

Jonquis' state of health did not seem to be improving. The doctor, who in the past tended to many battle wounds, was dealing with infection spread by a rabid animal. Who knows where that fox contracted its madness?

The day passed and Enyja kept vigil by his bedside. Jonquis was cold one moment and seemed to burning up the next. She dried his sweaty forehead with a damp cloth she wrung out in a pan of water. She was on hand to pull the bed blanket over him when he was cold. Jonquis mostly slept but did wake for food and drink, what little he did consume. It was very important for him to be drinking fluids to keep flushing his body. Not only was it difficult to swallow, but Jonquis much preferred to fall into the comfort of sleep. As Jonquis slept and she was sure that she was alone with him, Enyja kissed his lips.

Within two days of being summoned, the alchemist, Calogerus, had arrived from his home deep in the forest. Calogerus knew that the king would not summon him without a good reason. Upon examining Jonquis, he knew that the boy's condition was very serious. He would have preferred to see the boy immediately after the ordeal. Calogerus recognized what would neutralize the spread of this disease. He immediately assessed that the brewing of a tea would help. He realized there would be a special root that he would have to collect for its brewing. Calogerus called for the cook to make a soup heavy in salt and garlic. He asked for raw garlic cloves as well. When the garlic cloves arrived, Calogerus took a knife and cut a clove in half. He then rubbed it directly into the wound. He did that prior to setting out for the special root. Enyja was fearful for Jonquis; she did not like the smell of the garlic on the open wound. Dressed in a dark tunic with cloak, a walking stick, dark features on his skin and lines on his forehead, Calogerus appeared to be rather scary. She gathered the courage to speak to Calogerus and asked, "Is he going to die?"

There was silence; Enyja had tears in her eyes. Calogerus was not used to being addressed by youth; he had no patience for folly. He especially could not bear folly in adults. He did not speak much to anyone. He did speak and council her father the king, but to address a youth?

He looked at her with examining eyes and observed her future. Calogerus could see what lay ahead for both these children. For now he sensed that she was truly distressed over the young boy. Calogerus thought he might comfort her with a few well-chosen words, so he turned to her and replied, "No."

Calogerus then left to find the important root. It was not long before he returned with it. The special drink that was brewed did make a difference in Jonquis' condition.

Jonquis did slowly recover from his ordeal and both he and Enyja fell in love. They could not bare to be apart and had more correspondence than their respective parents the dukes. They yearned for the next visit at court that meant they could see each other. They thought that they were secretly sending letters to each other, but their romance was common knowledge to their respective servants, who were amused with the two. Later Jonquis and Enyja would marry and unite their two dukedoms into the kingdom of Craigroyston. The new coat of arms included the ram of Roysford and the anchor and cross of Craigton. Betrand could not be more grateful to Cardem and Calogerus. Calogerus, true to his form, slipped away to his forest home without delay. He did not stay long enough to be thanked for his part in helping Jonquis recover. It seemed that Calogerus was not a sociable individual. Nevertheless, Enyja would make it a task to find Calogerus' dwelling place and thank him properly.

A few days had passed and Jonquis was restored to health. Enyja was so happy that Jonquis was well. Since Jonquis had not been in a proper state of health to receive Calogerus, Enyja told him everything. She suggested that they should ride out and properly say thank you to him. She told him all about Calogerus, how he was dressed, how he appeared and disappeared and how she planned to ride out and find him. Jonquis had quite enough adventure.

"I thought that you told me that it took two days for him to get here?" questioned Jonquis. However, at the bidding of Enyja, Jonquis would do anything.

"Two days on foot; we have horses," Enyja replied confidently.

It was hard to believe. Despite their recent ordeal, they set out into the forest to search for the dwelling place of Calogerus. They did not know where this place was, only that he lived somewhere out deep in the forest. Enyja remembered her father telling Yonny to take the west road to the forest fence. King Cardem had a special horn that could summon Calogerus. Even though Enyja knew about the horn, she respected the fact that it should only be used for urgent matters.

Betrand had to return to Craigton, but he more than trusted Jonquis in Cardem's house. Betrand left behind a party of capable servants to accompany Jonquis back home when he was well enough to travel. When Tonio, Betrand's emissary, went to check on Jonquis, he was not there. He soon learned that Enyja was nowhere to be found either. Tonio approached Cardem to tell him of his discovery. It was wonderful that Jonquis was well enough to get out for fresh air, but where did Enyja and he go this time?

On this occasion the two youths prepared for their journey by removing food from the castle kitchen and bringing not only daggers but two bows with arrows, which both youths claimed to be experts with. The journey through the dark forest reminded them why it was referred to as the dark forest. The tall trees shaded the interior and their leaves soaked up the sun's rays. It was cool. As they ventured farther, there were thickets and vines all over with sharp pricks and the ground did not look disturbed. Even silence made a sound in this forest. Not many travellers took this route.

Nevertheless, after travelling on horseback and wandering the whole day, they were ready to give up and return. They would have returned but they got turned around and lost their direction. As it grew darker, they saw a light that emanated from a lamp. They dismounted and quietly walked their fine horses toward the lamp. The lamp was on a post that lit a charming little cottage in the distance. In an instant from behind them appeared a large, cloaked man equipped to do battle. The figure was menacing and their fear sent them pacing backward until Jonquis tripped back and fell to the ground. Enyja immediately crouched down beside him fearing the worst. Then the dark cloaked figure, who recognized who the trespassers were, removed his head cover. It was Calogerus.

If the look on the two travellers had been of fear, they were relieved to see Calogerus. Calogerus, of course, posed a look of surprise at seeing these two youngsters so far from home when they had recently had a perilous adventure. Calogerus, for his part, was actually pleased to see them. He could foresee their future. He was flattered that they had sought him. He took them inside his house. Although quaint, this cottage was very far away from any neighbour. People had to work together in a community. Calogerus often professed the advantages of people uniting, yet he himself lived in recluse. The dwelling served Calogerus well and gave him peace and quiet to study plants, animals and minerals; yet he was alone.

Calogerus was a wise man with powers to see into the future. He was born with this special gift and he cultivated it. The truth is, the further back one looked, he was sure to see what he was to face anyway. Calogerus just paid more attention to the details. The ability to read life experiences and the power to use common sense equipped this man with what was perceived as magic. To a common man, a little common sense was like magic. His mother was skilled at dressing and healing wounds that the fighting men incurred during battle. Calogerus was introduced to all manner of alchemy and herbal knowledge at a rather young age. It was rumoured that his father had been a great warrior known as the "Grey Knight." The "Grey Knight" served the old Duke Gwyndor, Cardem's father.

When his father died, Calogerus, a very young boy, went with his mother to live in the Duke's castle. Calogerus got to know Cardem very well, and he developed a loyalty to him. Although Calogerus was awkward, Cardem treated him nicely and stood up for him in the company of other pompous boys and girls. Calogerus never forgot about Cardem's kindness. The young Cardem grew into a man and became Duke of Roysford at the passing of his father, Gwyndor. Through his special sensitivity, Calogerus had the ability to look into the future. He could read people's hearts. He could feel when the seasons changed and whether there would be harsh weather.

During a harvest feast at the castle one year, there was a bounty of food and drink. There was boasting and waste and this ingratitude Calogerus could not stand. He knew this condition of bounty would not last forever. Calogerus counselled Cardem to store more grain in the bountiful years to offset poorer crop yields that he saw coming. Cardem built another granary and rotated the stock in compliance. "Keep the trough full" was Calogerus' advice. Calogerus even suggested burying cabbage and turnips in tarpaulins about knee deep into the ground so the winter frost would keep them from rotting. It turned out that he was right. The lean years came. The idea of burying cabbage just before winter to prolong its use became a way of storing food that would normally perish long before spring. The food was used when the spring sun thawed the ground, making it accessible again. In lean years, pick axes were used to remove the frozen soil and get at the cabbage well before spring. Calogerus not only had vision but the wisdom to construe what to do.

In an ironic turn of events, Calogerus was blinded by the affection of a maiden whom he fell in love with. Never ask Calogerus if love is blind. They were married and she bore him a child. One day when he returned from Cardem's court, they were gone. There was no trace. It nearly drove him mad and he could not speak. He abandoned his home and plot of land, and retreated to the forest and within himself. To this day he still lives deep in the forest.

Calogerus scolded the two youths but it did not take long before he prepared a meal for the weary travellers. They seemed to fill a void for company in his life. For even a man with a brilliant mind needs to be included in someone's life. Enyja would not only impress Calogerus, but gain a trusted, respected advisor for her and Jonquis in their future. Their two dukedoms would unite and become one kingdom namely through advice Calogerus put forth to Cardem and Betrand.

For his part, Calogerus would come to love Enyja and Jonquis as though they were his own children. Of course he never let on in his direct candour and demeanour. As for Enyja and Jonquis, they had a feeling of love and respect toward Calogerus. They respected his advice and they would see their kingdom prosper with his help. Through Calogerus' wisdom, Craigroyston would gain respect from its neighbours and gain access to gates that were once closed to it. Craigroyston also formed alliances with noble neighbours and honoured these accords. They did not hesitate to come to the aid of a neighbour against treachery. During the rule of Jonquis and Enyja, Calogerus would work tirelessly to ensure their reign would be one of justice, fairness, peace and prosperity. For now, Jonquis and Enyja were good company.

Lessons from the Past

In Rothaynen, Brandyn's service to Woodcroft not only took form in the ways of learning the sword, axe, lance and horsemanship, but in the form of education as well. There were a full twenty-four hours in a day, and Woodcroft made time to educate Brandyn so he could read and write. The ability to read was empowering. Not everybody could read the written word. It was a welcome skill that could improve the human condition. Woodcroft believed that every child should have the opportunity that he himself had, to learn how to read. Every great nation had writing and art to record their history and pass down stories of great heroism in the struggle for justice and truth. At first Brandyn was excited about reading and learning to write his own name. What he learned was that it took time and effort. Woodcroft continued to encourage his young protege until he could actually make out the letters that Brandyn had scratched on the page. At one instance it looked as though Brandyn put ink on a chicken's feet and had the fowl walk across the page. In the absence of anything else, at least Brandyn was willing to try, and he did improve. Brandyn could now read and write a little.

Woodcroft liked to discuss history and its politics. Woodcroft was a servant of God, king and country, but he realized even people with great power can make errors in judgment. Despite the raids from outside the kingdom, sometimes enemies were found within a kingdom. Overlords were ready to betray the people for some personal gain having struck and alliance with another warring lord. "Even a good king has enemies and traitors," confided Woodcroft. "There are those who are never happy. The weak king betrays himself because mismanagement results in hunger, poverty and lack of justice. The result of poor stewardship are uprisings. It opens the door for power struggles."

"So you are arguing that a king should be firm and strong and not afraid to rule with absolute power?" questioned Brandyn.

"If a king were to rule with an iron hand, that would not be good either. The people would live in fear of expressing their ideas. There are tyrants who think only of themselves and have no regard for the people they oppress. Eventually the people could unite against him and overthrow him. Let me ask you. Would it be wrong to oppose a bad king? If people live in fear and are oppressed by their overseers, and if it were for the good of the kingdom to replace their king, would that be just cause to overthrow him?" he challenged Brandyn.

"You should always support your king," was Brandyn's firm reply. "God would expect you to do your duty faithfully, honourably and show loyalty."

"You mean well, Brandyn, but what if the king is wrong and his decision will bring death to you and the men who are in your care?"

That was a difficult question. Brandyn always listened to Woodcroft when he discussed politics. Brandyn asked questions when he did not understand. There were many questions. Governing people successfully seemed to depend on providing a reliable supply of food. Brandyn learned that politics was so easy and yet so hard to understand.

For an example, Woodcroft told him the story of a famous battle that had taken place. Not long ago, a campaign was fought over Sadar, an ambitious war lord from Peregren, which was located just northwest of Braemar. The region was rich in iron deposits that were mined and hence home to blacksmiths who forged weapons. For these strategic reasons and location, Peregren was King Lyndorn's original castle. King Lyndorn was the father of Orendyn and grandfather of the present King Graedon. All sorts of military weapons and gear from archers arrows, swords, armour, lances and spears were all fashioned in the "pits of Peregren" where the fires of their furnaces were rumoured never to go out. Sadar convinced the grumbling landlords, barons and counts in his region to join him. Given their castle at Peregren, and endless resources of armaments and fighting men, he argued that they were secure. With the vicinity of Marmora's gardens and fruit orchards, they were self-sufficient in Peregren. Why should they pay tribute to finance Orendyn's heir, the new King Graedon in his new castle at Braemar?

Sadar argued that the other dukes and their armies, in fact the entire kingdom of Rothaynen, depended on Peregren armaments. It was in their power to cut off the supply of armaments which would make them at Peregren invincible. Who then would dare oppose them at Peregren?

When they fought battles in the other parts of the kingdom, reinforcements were late, if they arrived at all. When it was time to claim the spoils though, they all wanted their share. They even joined in the celebration afterwards by filling their bellies with food and drink. They paraded about as conquering warriors. Sadar made a good case because Peregren was nestled away safely behind the mountains and had not been attacked for a hundred years. Depending on where the battle was and where you had to come from, Sadar's argument could be made by anyone. Sadar knew how to incite the grumbling landlords. Some people do not know when their cup is full. Sadar promised them a better life. The argument was put forth that this present alliance was not to their advantage. The taxes on their woodlands and armaments that were sent to the king in tribute could better be used at their discretion and in their region. Sadar did not support Orendyn's heir. He grumbled against Orendyn's rule; why would he support his son?

Sadar's actual goal was to break away from young Graedon's rule by rallying other disgruntled nobles with his rabble rousing. This new accord would then march into the heart of Rothaynen and capture the new Braemar Castle. They would depose Graedon and bring a new order that would make him, Sadar, the new king.

Of course, Graedon, his court and his army depended on his landlord's loyalty. The produce from Marmora was meant to be distributed fairly throughout the kingdom. The collection of taxes from every subject helped to sustain the entire kingdom. Graedon could not let the rebels secede and use their resources against the rest of dukes in the kingdom. They had to oppose the rebels. Graedon called on Barton and Welledon. The force from Braemar Castle, whose construction was not entirely complete, were joined by those of Barton of Teresforte, with Welledon of Galles trailing by a day. Sadar had not counted on Graedon, Barton and Welledon mobilizing so quickly. If there had been a major assault from the sea on Barton's castle, Petrinvincit, there would be very few left to defend it. Barton's entire force was moving swiftly across Marmora to Peregren at the behest of Graedon.

Fortunately, Sadar's alliance made up mostly of disgruntled nobles, farmers and idle sluggards, basked with confidence in their weapons. They were very slow to ready for war. The mobilization of Graedon's army and the twin forces of Barton and Welledon was quick because they knew that Sadar had the resources. They did not want to give Sadar time to prepare and organize his force. Graedon's forces were so quick, they were able to divide Sadar's forces and face the allied warring lords separately and defeat them. In the confusion, Sadar himself was killed by his mistress' son, whom he had promoted to his court from a page to squire and then knight. Sadar had despised the child from the moment he met him, but he had fallen in love with his mother. Graedon recognized that knight from when he was a squire the day Sadar had assisted his father, King Orendyn, at Teresforte.

Many years before, there was a misunderstanding between his father Orendyn and his uncle Arlenden, when a siege was laid on Petrinvincit. Graedon remembered how Sadar was upset when he did not get promoted. Instead, he humiliated this young squire needlessly before all to see. Graedon, who was prince at the time, took note of Sadar's attitude and his mistreatment of the squire. The squire did not deserve that beating. The squire was rumoured to be his son, but Sadar referred to him as a bastard. Sadar loved his mother but would not marry her. He hated that the boy was the son from another man, who obviously did not care. He just wanted his mother. What choice did his mother have to turn down Sadar's advances?

The young man was Lucio. No more would Sadar insult, deride and punish the boy. Graedon replaced all who challenged his authority in the Peregren court with loyal nobles. With all that ill treatment, derision and bullying, Lucio learned a great deal about politics—at a very young age.

What transpired at Peregren was the senseless loss of good fighting men. Even more bloodshed could have occurred if Graedon's forces had not acted so quickly. A good leader was what was needed. A new leader for Peregren was appointed by Graedon. He was not from the Peregren region but a loyal, trustworthy young captain from Teresforte. Barton had great admiration for his captain, whose character and deeds were well known to Graedon. The people of Peregren would answer to Federics. Graedon felt that any resentment against appointing an "outsider" to the region would quell after the region was well-managed and prospered. People were willing to forget if things got better. Besides, Federics would have the young Lucio to assist him. It was not long before Federics also fell in love with the boy's mother, Vanessa.

Woodcroft always discussed matters of politics with Brandyn. "The king depends on his lord's loyalty and sense of fairness and justice in dealing with his subjects. A king cannot be everywhere. If there is selfishness on the part of the overlords, you come to realize that the rebellious subjects may have reason, and good reason, for their grievance. Nevertheless, it was not wise to have a king overrule his landlords should they make the odd error in judgment on domestic affairs. Making mistakes is easy, but what you do after you learn that you were wrong is what determines character. That is why the knights were summoned to police his majesty's kingdom. They were given the right to bear arms and mete justice in the land. It was their duty to vanquish ignorance, oppression and selfishness, foremost within themselves. Sometimes the landlords and knights could be at odds. It was vital that a trust be in place. Trust is a high principle and most necessary to the success of governing people, and yet who could you trust? In these dark times, people lived in fear."

Woodcroft concluded, "So the quarrels, treacheries and the struggle for justice continued. You cannot say that we attained justice and 'there we are done.' Where there is a will to promote justice, the chances for injustice are reduced—not eliminated. In short, if the motives of those who govern are good and the people are willing to work and be productive, then the kingdom prospers. It is when we sit back and care not that we lose. It is when we allow evil ideas to prosper without account, that we lose. It is when the mighty inflict their will over the people by force, that we lose. All people, not just knights, need to be on guard and vigilant for truth and justice."

Woodcroft's ideas were always good willed and of high ideal.

The Beast of Burden

An example of Woodcroft's grievance resolution occurred when the grains were gathered for shipment to the granaries that very harvest at Wendover. Woodcroft and Brandyn were too happy to be there, each with the girl of their dreams. The forces were preparing to go home after the defeat of the Huynstens. That summer, the lack of natural rainfall more specifically affected the oat crop, which did not yield the anticipated quota. Senus, the king's tax collector, was insistent on collecting the full 143 vessels of oats, leaving the farmers with barely enough to seed the fields next spring let alone enough to feed their families. The agreement called for 143 vessels and the remainder would be kept by the farmer who could use, sell and reseed. With the soldiers presence, there was very little anyone could do about the matter. However, the entire Wendover area was short on most estimated quotas that year. After having supported the king's soldiers in the area, the tribute to Craigroyston in gratitude for Selwyck's service, damages from the raiding and burning and the weather conditions that season, could the king's collectors not understand that the quota should be relaxed?

The king's soldiers themselves witnessed the harvests, the thrashing, the storage in the barns. There was no scheme to cheat the landlord from his portion. Surely there could be a reasonable allowance made so that the settlements would be fair.

The collectors merely argued the responsibility of the king to allocate fairly the grain so that all his subjects could enjoy their portion. The following could only happen if all quotas were collected. They were bent on keeping to the letter of the agreement. The issue really ignited when the senior collector stressed that the people should be more conservative with their consumption. It was not very diplomatic.

At that the people cried out that it was the king's armies who helped themselves to anything and everything. They ate so much it was doubtful they could do battle after gorging themselves the way they did. They never replaced the timber from fences that they took. They used the wood to light fires to keep warm in their encampments in the cooler autumn nights. They just plain took things for granted. They were idle most of the time while the people worked hard. Besides, the farmers were forced by law to build bridges over streams that ran across their property so the king's soldiers could mobilize for their defence more effectively.

It was Woodcroft to the rescue. Before there was a formal uprising, in which some farmers would fight valiantly and die, Woodcroft chose to intervene. As a knight he was able to hear the grievance put forth by the farmers. Woodcroft was aware that the king's granaries worked on the principle of maintaining reserves, so there was no immediate crisis. In order to unite the people behind their king, it was important to deal fairly to promote the smooth operation of next years crop and harvest. The present year did prove to be a little disappointing due to weather. After he drew the attention of the angry farmers and the stone-faced, unrelenting tax collectors to himself, he hopped up on a wagon, which was laden with grain, and began to recount a story. The story was a guide for managing servants with fairness. This was a story his father told him when he was a little boy. Coming from a privileged family meant that there was a lot to be grateful for and it should not be taken for granted. Just like there are rights and responsibilities associated with the farmers and trades people, so are there with the privileged overlords. Welledon's lineage in Galles, to the southwest of the kingdom, strove to be fair and just stewards of the land. Their reputation for fairness and justice preceded them.

Woodcroft began his story. "There was a man who owned a donkey. He did not own very much land to speak of, just enough to keep a few animals and grow a modest amount of grain. He earned most of his money transporting other people's stock and wares to the village. He was often payed in grain, which he sold along with any of his own for silver coins."

"Did he get sheared by the tax collectors too?" interrupted an angry farmer. The comment gathered moans and a mocking laugh, but Woodcroft continued.

"He wanted to be a smarter man and he thought on the idea. He reasoned if he consumed less, then there would be more to add to his profits. He lived miserly and expected his donkey to do the same."

As Woodcroft continued his story, he captivated everyone as they waited to hear what came next.

"He reduced the donkey's feed and realized that the work that the donkey performed was the same. This, of course, was more profitable, and since the donkey did not sense any difference, he concluded that it was a very smart move. After a whole week the man thought on the idea of reducing the donkey's feed a little more. Again, the donkey performed his routine work, although he appeared a little more tired. He reasoned that the donkey could rest in the down time that the winter provided after the harvest. He seemed to have it all worked out. The plan made sense, it was reasonable and what is more, it was working. The man continued to reduce the donkey's grain yet another time. In this instance it was not to yield the results he expected. When he went to his barn, he found that the donkey had died. So who would now do the work of a beast of burden?"

"Why, the 'other' jackass, of course!" heckled one of the farmers, to which the crowd broke out into laughter.

Needless to say, the tax collectors were not amused. However, at Woodcroft's bidding, a new settlement was negotiated and agreed to by the farmers and Senus, the chief tax collector. Woodcroft had earned the respect of the farmers as a just and fair administrator of the king's affairs. The chief tax collector did not share the same feeling. Senus saw himself as representing the crown, and he had been put on trial by the peasants. It was not really the case since common sense merely prevailed. Nevertheless, he would later report the affair to Lucio when he returned to Braemar Castle. Lucio had moved to Braemar Castle. Lucio gained favour with the king over the passing years due to the successful service to Federics in Peregren. Since Federics had always spoken highly of Lucio, his request was granted. As of late he resided in Braemar and sat at the king's court. His mother, Vanessa, had moved with him.

Upon being knighted, the king himself reminded his subject that the duties of a knight are to vanquish ignorance, oppression and selfishness. Brandyn got to observe the many cases that Woodcroft heard that involved civil law. In civil law a citizen can have a grievance against another citizen or their landlord. He learned that Woodcroft was not only a mighty warrior and learned man, but a very wise knight.

Life Giving Water in Scales of Justice

In one case, in the Gallesian fields where watering rights were to be shared, a man was killed over a dispute. The local magistrate was going to try the man, Vaille, for the murder of Thombs. This capital offence would be punishable by death. Woodcroft, who happened to be in the area, was approached by Vaille's wife, who pleaded for her husband's life. Upon hearing her story, he learned that it was Thombs who had not shut his water-access gate to allow for the water to reach Vaille's farm. Without water, the crops they depended on would naturally wither and die. Without crops for winter, his family would wither and die as well. This was not the first time he had to remind Thombs about shutting the water-access gate. When Vaille approached Thombs this time, Thombs, being a huskier man, began to intimidate and push him. He began with words but push came to shove and Vaille was knocked to the ground. While Thombs reached for some wood to scare Vaille, Vaille had found a rock from being on the ground. In the panic that ensued, Vaille struck the attacking Thombs in the crest on his head. The blow was enough to kill the man.

Woodcroft interviewed other neighbouring farmers for a character sketch of the two men. After questioning them, Woodcroft ruled that the case was a simple matter of self-defence. There was no intent to kill. The circumstances were mitigated by the discourteousness of Thombs, which the other farmers attested to. It was important that the people of the area be heard after all. Vaille would still have to live there and face his neighbours from day to day. It seemed that the people of the village agreed with Woodcroft's decision, since Thombs bullying was not exclusive to Vaille. The magistrate was forced to acquit and release Vaille of murder but assessed a penalty to compensate Thombs' widow. Since Thombs' children were young girls, Vaille would be responsible for the caring and harvesting of Thombs' farm that autumn. In spring, he would assist with planting until such time that Thombs' spouse or daughters married. Since Vaille had boys of his own, they could help out too.

Beloved Son

It was nearly a month since the thwarted Huynsten invasion of Wendover took place. In that time Brandyn had witnessed the gore and glory of battle, and the strife of civil discord. Time, like the water that flows to the sea, passes incessantly. In that same time Brandyn had grown taller and stronger and wiser. Brandyn went with Woodcroft to meet Welledon at Galles whenever their policing allowed them to visit. The castle of Welledon was protectorate for the Gallesian fields. The area was too rocky to be a specialized farming place such as Wendover, but there was some mixed farming. Red potatoes were grown everywhere as a staple by the farmers. They even terraced them on the fertile plains on the mountain sides. There was an abundance of slate, which is lightweight stone that looks greyish blue. When layered, slate is very useful for sheathing roofs. The material is strong and durable. The abundance of natural sandstone rock made it ideal for stone masons to quarry their supply of stone for building. The Gallesian fields had some of the prettiest stone cottages with slate roofs that you could imagine. The stone masons of the Gallesian fields were among the finest anywhere, as the look and endurance of their communities attested to. Galles Castle was nestled inside the mountain region of the southwest. It was a splendid fortress with artistic beauty that was a credit to its builders and craftsmen.

Woodcroft, the only living heir of Lord Welledon of Galles, now courted Brandyn's sister. Although not official, each were intended for each other. The two could see each other whenever the king's affairs allowed Woodcroft to frequent Wendover. In a relatively short period Woodcroft and Brandyn developed a close trust and friendship. Woodcroft considered Brandyn his younger brother. Woodcroft had an older brother, Bram, who was as fine a knight as could be found. He tragically met his death in battle in the pursuit of saving his own father. In the very midst of battle, Bram left his opponent to confront attackers that were teaming his father. Bram threw his sword at the stomach of a third warrior that was attacking his father from behind. Although he saved his father, Bram, without his sword, was pursued and stabbed in the back. At seeing Bram's death, Welledon's forces redoubled their efforts and routed the mercenaries. Welledon was heartbroken; he had the company of two fine boys at his table and he had lost Bram. When Brandyn arrived at Galles, he was a welcome member at Welledon's table. He had never gotten used to losing his son Bram, but the boy's presence comforted him. Having Brandyn there made breaking bread more complete.

The other young pages and squires accepted Brandyn too. This young upstart weathered their pranks and the normal welcome they gave all new squires. Even Lucio, who was making a name for himself, was interested in winning over Brandyn as well. During that year, Brandyn had earned the respect and approval of many of the king's lords. Among them, Lord Barton, whom the king entrusted like his own brother, was impressed with Brandyn's enthusiasm.

Invincible Rock: Thicker Than Blood

In actuality, King Graedon and Lord Barton were cousins. A generation earlier their fathers were brothers. The elder Orendyn inherited, upon the death of his father, Lyndorn, the castle at Peregren and the lands of Rothaynen. Although his castle was at Peregren, he chose to start constructing a new castle that was more central in Rothaynen. The castle was to be built southeast of there on Thermanden Bay at the far east end of the River Brae. In his wisdom and love for his younger brother Arlenden, he thought he too should have his own castle. Arlenden could live as a king himself and they could protect the gardens and orchards of Marmora and expand on the lands their father entrusted to their stewardship. Besides, Orendyn thought that a castle fortress built at the mouth of the River Brae to the west, could stand as a great protector for the kingdom from any army that threatened to attack him farther inland at Braemar. If a siege were attempted at Braemar Castle in the heart of Rothaynen, the force from Teresforte would come to their aid. It would be an assurance having another fortified castle at the other end of their garden country. If an enemy force arrived at Teresforte, the strong castle would stand until the force from Braemar came to their aid. It would be like playing the two knights in a game of chess strategically. The plan was perfect.

The invincible castle was to be built high atop the rocky mountains at the mouth of the River Brae. The castle would overlook the Verdent Salt Sea and stand as a natural fortress. The castle was indeed a splendour in stone masonry. It provided the strength and prestige that a kingdom aspired to. It was beautiful and created constructive work for years to come. Let us assume for the moment that the castle at Teresforte was not built. Because of its location, the sea that carved its fingers against the rock creating crevices, fjords and sharp rubble of all sizes, the water levels you could not judge and the constant barrage of water cascading against the rock, it might be entertaining to see anyone try to land there. In fact, if you could throw a stone, you could defend Pertrinvincit. It was the name that Orendyn gave his brother's castle. The name means "invincible rock." During its construction, Petrinvincit was attacked on five separate occasions and all five times Arlenden's men left their constructing and repelled the attacker. During the fourth of these attacks, it was revealed to Arlenden that the greatest vulnerability was the eastern side. It was the castle's only vulnerability. What if an army was landed up river and circled around and attacked from the farmlands?

The sea to the west would work against him while a siege was conducted from the farmland to the east. That army would also have the food of the farmland while the forces inside the castle starved. On the eastern side of the castle lay Marmora's farmland and orchards that stretched out toward the east. Arlenden commissioned a stone wall to be built around the perimeter of the castle's east side, including the south shore. This stone wall would surely slow down if not stop an enemy force. It took nearly twenty more years to complete the wall. The thick stone walls were quarried from the coastal mountains so the material was not only available but close by. On the northern side, they only needed to bridge the mountain passes between the natural barriers that the bedrock provided.

By this time Orendyn was made suspicious of his brother's efforts by his council. It was the king's advisors that were actually distrustful, but the seed was planted. When Orendyn sent an emissary to Arlenden's court, they were met with less than a warm welcome, but not by Arlenden. Some of Arlelnden's close advisors had ideas of their own and mistreated Orendyn's emissary, who promptly returned to report to Orendyn. In all fairness, Orendyn's royal emissary was rather pompous too because he did not stay long enough to meet with Arlenden. Upon his return, the feeling in Orendyn's court was that the situation was treasonous. There was an all-out summoning of the king's armies, who gathered in Marmora at the plains of Lyndendor, just east of Teresforte. The assault on Petrinvincit took place well before the encircling wall was finished. King Orendyn gathered an overwhelming force. Part of that force from Peregren, under their captain Sadar, slipped around and through portions of the mountain where the wall was not yet built. When Arlenden was alerted to the coming force, he had no intention to fight against his brother. He did not order a mobilization of his soldiers and defences. Arlenden forbade his archers to fire upon his brother's army. Sadar's army in the higher mountain pass would have been annihilated if the archers attacked with their arrows from high atop the fortified castle. In fact, a constant wave of arrows from the castle ramparts could have seriously pared Orendyn's forces. Unfortunately, there were ambitious nobles and knights in his court that sought to overthrow Arlenden. They would gladly see Teresforte as a separate kingdom independent of Rothaynen. It would seem that there had been just cause for Orendyn's advisors to suspect treason.

And so with everyone prepared for battle, a group of Arlenden's knights started to attack the king's men on the plains before the castle. In open battle Arlenden's men were no match for Orendyn's hardened, experienced, disciplined land force. Arlenden did not order them to attack. The men who perished that day at the hands of Orendyn's force did so at the bidding of the ambitious, rebel knights led by Luddex. After seeing the provocation from the highlands, Sadar ordered his forces from Peregren to attack from the north. He had his archers set fire to the north castle gate. The archers and soldiers inside were a little nervous since they were ordered not to fire upon Orendyn's forces. Luckily, the castle gate was thick. There, Sadar waited behind the mountain walls for the thick gate to be consumed by fire so he could enter with his forces. Sadar thought that if he could capture the castle, Orendyn would reward his bravery handsomely. From within the safety of the castle, Arlenden and his trusted knights rode out of the main gate to see his brother under a flag of truce. Although they were not armed for battle, they were nearly attacked themselves. Mattews and Winn, two loyal, young knights of Orendyn, recognized the king's brother and his intentions. They both led a wave of Orendyn's army between Arlenden's men and Sadar's forces that rushed down from the mountain heights to engage them in battle. Sadar knew full well that Arlenden had come out under a flag of truce.

In the end, the damage could have been even worse by way of bloodshed, as two forces serving the same house were deceived into believing that they were enemies. Had Arlenden taken earlier action, mobilized his defences and ordered a full attack against his brother's forces, there would have been no winner that day. There had been some carnage on the plains that day. The beautiful carving on the great north gate of Petrinvincit was set afire and burned, that is, what was capable of burning. The thick gate got damaged. The castle was mostly rock. The wood carvers and carpenters that fashioned the gate to remarkable beauty and prestige would have to be recalled though.

Orendyn pledged to repair the damage to his brother's house using the wealth forfeited by the rebel nobles and knights and traitors who perpetrated the disaster that nearly cost him his brother and his kingdom. This was the beginning of Sadar's grumbling against Orendyn. Sadar had expected to be rewarded with a better title. He was dreaming of acquiring the title of Lord of Teresforte or Lord of Peregren, since the king planned to build himself a new castle. Instead, he witnessed a reconciliation between the two brothers. He took his anger out on his squire, as he had often done.

He lost his temper over some triviality and beat the squire to the ground. He would later oppose Orendyn's son, Graedon, because he did not get his share of the prize that day. Orendyn further angered Sadar when he learned that he was staying at Peregren, the new castle on Thermanden Bay to be given to Graedon. The new edifice would be named Braemar Castle. Although at Orendyn's death Sadar was named steward in Peregren due to appease his steadfast service, it was not enough for him.

Both Orendyn and Arlenden realized the power of tyranny and what might have happened. So did Lucio, who was a serf under Sadar's command. These individuals saw how a single moment could consume all that it took years to build. The brothers were not only thinking of Petrinvincit but reflected on their growing up together as trusting brothers, with the same mother and father. Sadar's squire Lucio, who had been humiliated before Peregren's army, had learned a lot as well. He learned how important the ability to communicate was. He saw how greed, trickery, ambition and lack of communication could cause rock to crumble. The two brothers pondered the same lesson. They questioned, "how had it come to this?"

Although the guilty were punished, innocent people died too. Since that fateful day, no enemy force has ever breached Petrinvincit or set fire to its gates. Braemar Castle never saw an enemy force come to its walls either. Rothaynen now looked to add Wendover and Mead to its realm. All Graedon had to do was to provide protection for these people and promote fair trade. The family succession has been loyal to the task of governing a united people with justice for all.

Noble Neighbor

Rothaynen seemed to have settled its problems with internal strife. But the real prize that year came when the mighty Welledon, Duke of Galles, declared his allegiance to King Orendyn. It was a cold winter that year, and even colder when you lacked food. The generosity of Orendyn and Arlenden rescued Welledon's subjects in Galles from starvation, as their potato crop fell victim to blight that fall harvest. Welledon could well have fought and conquered for what his people needed. His skilled army and people were willing to do anything but starve. Welledon, however, was a noble warrior, a fair and just man, in seeing his neighbour's good faith and generosity, he joined his people to Rothaynen.

Ambitions

It was not until the untimely death of Woodcroft in the defence of the Mead coast that Brandyn began to feel ill at ease with Lucio. When Graedon summoned knights from Peregren in mid-summer, Federics put his ward Lucio in charge. Lucio had prospered under his guidance and that of his mother Vanessa. Federics was captivated by Vanessa's eloquence, wisdom and beauty. She was older than Federics; just how old was hard to say, but she had breeding. Federics put Lucio in charge of his forces for land defence. This, he thought, would not only impress Lucio but his mother as well. It did not impress the chain of command. There were other qualified knights for the task who contributed longer, were older and more experienced than Lucio. It was Federics' will, though, that Lucio be put in command. The other men honoured Federics' wishes because he had earned their respect. Federics always ruled the people of Peregren with their welfare in mind. When fisherman in Mead observed a small group of Orgol ships, they reported it to Dane, a knight of Mead. The Orgol ships were indecisive about attacking. While scouting down the coast, Shirewynn, another knight of Mead, saw that more Orgol ships were coming; he reported back to Graedon. The Orgol ships may have been separated by a storm at sea. Graedon, who had previously dispatched Woodcroft to join Mead's force, added Lucio's force from Peregren for assurance. The forces to defend Mead had arrived with plenty of time.

It is true that Woodcroft died at the hands of the enemy that day. The retreating enemy doubled back after leading a handful of the king's knights, without proper accompaniment, into an ambush. Even the archers did not support them. With all Brandyn had observed over the many battles he saw, it was not necessary. The battle had turned in their favour. They were well reinforced by Peregren, and the enemy, who came from the sea, had no means of resupplying itself. All they had to do was hold their ground and wait for the enemy to board their vessels and sail away. Even after the ambush on Woodcroft's force, there was no offensive to avenge the fallen knights. Woodcroft, Dane and Shirewynn would never charge out without proper support. Something had gone wrong. The forces from inland Mead just watched the Orgols retreat with their wares and weapons, and disappear on the cloudy sea.

However, unknown to common knowledge, it was most necessary to Lucio's plan to extend his influence and power over the king's armies. Lucio had been in discussion with his colleagues, and they agreed on a plan. The forces in land at Mead were prepared and ready. Lucio signalled the advance for ten soldiers led by three knights, Woodcroft, Dane and Shirewynn to advance. They advanced to certain death. Part of the plan that was agreed on, was not carried out. With the loss of those distinguished and respected knights, Lucio's position would grow stronger. Who else would be in line for promotion?

Lucio had planned on usurping the loyalty of the army and all the new young knights to perceive him and him alone as the first captain and military advisor to King Graedon. It was Lucio who would make the reports and converse directly with Graedon. It was Lucio who would tell the army what the will of the king was. It was Lucio who would direct battles from a safe place while he sent others into the path of harm. Lucio was elevated to the king's personal body guard and was thus responsible for security at Braemar Castle and the court. He would actually be privy to important information at the moment the king received it. Lucio could therefore increase his influence over the lords, nobles and knights and even the king. And then who else would challenge him for the hand of the princess, and more importantly in Lucio's eyes, the crown?

And that was just the beginning.

It would be very hard to go against a man who had the army at his command. It would only be a matter of time before all the older lords would die off, leaving Lucio to influence what happened to their estates, who could marry their widows, and shape all of the younger, ambitious, inexperienced lords, nobles and knights to his plans. Lucio could indoctrinate them to be copies of himself so they would love no one else but he. He recently gave Todden, a knight that was aged 38, the hand of a wealthy widow ten years his senior. Todden had not met the widow. All that he knew was that she was wealthy and that he would be the Lord of Dumfresen. That was all that Todden needed to know. The widow, for her part, had no choice. She believed that it was Graedon's will that she marry Todden. She did so to keep her status, order and peace. Lucio was clever, careful and calculating in learning all that he could before acting. Indeed, what Sadar had tried to accomplish with force, Lucio was achieving with Graedon's seal of approval. At least it was perceived that way. A king's messenger can only be doing the will of the king after all.

Noble Words

It was Lucio who made a moving speech at the burial rights of Woodcroft, Dane and Shirewynn.

"Our brothers have fallen, not in vain, however, for they knew it was their duty to serve and protect the dear people of Mead. We can rejoice in their fearless heroism and example they gave on how a life should be led. Their selfless sacrifice will not only have served to protect those who could not protect themselves, but serve as an example to all of us, especially the knights, squires and pages who will keep this example in their hearts when the time comes for them to take up arms and serve."

Lucio had craftily turned the sullen occasion into one of honour, hope and inspiration. By granting to the squires of the fallen knights, their sponsor's horse, sword, and armour, they became distracted with the notion. In the case of the fallen knights' rings that bore their respective seals, Lucio would personally see that they were taken back to their proper families. Woodcroft's ring that bore the seal of Galles, that Welledon gave his son, was removed off his finger by Lucio. Lucio would have an audience with these families and build a rapport with them. It was vitally important to meet Welledon, who was an influential and loyal man to Graedon. Welledon now lost his younger son, and there was no heir for Galles.

For the while, Lucio laid to rest any doubt of his true devotion to the knights who had fallen, and Brandon felt honoured that he should acquire Vento, Woodcroft's trusty steed, his sword and the armour that he had polished and kept for his lord. Lucio even said that he would speak to Welledon on his behalf. Despite the circumstances and despite the sense of sorrow, at last Brandyn would have the tools he needed to become a knight. He did not feel right about not going to see Welledon in person. He had broken bread at his table with Woodcroft like he was family. Before Brandyn could tell Lucio that he wanted to go along, Lucio had departed for Galles. The force from Galles stayed behind at Mead, but soldiers from Peregen and Braemar made their way to Braemar Castle.

Absent from Home

Upon their return to Braemar Castle, Brandyn trained along with the squires. A good number of them were sponsored by knights that were loyal to Lucio. Training for the joust really took concentration. After being caught in daydreaming a few times and being knocked off his horse, Brandyn became more alert. He began to focus more on the task at hand. The armour did not fit him perfectly. Brandyn's arms and legs were a little longer than Woodcroft's. On his return, Lucio saved the day by having the royal blacksmith fashion the suit to his dimensions. There was not that much that needed alteration. All the while his skill at the joust was improving. His arm grew stronger at wielding the lance. He got used to riding Vento, Woodcroft's horse, who was well skilled at the motions his former master had entrenched in him. The horse had the sense to react to the feel of his master's weight as it shifted in the saddle. Vento had a keen sense and perfect timing. Brandyn need only follow Vento's lead to be successful.

The other squires were, for the most part, competitive and fair except for a handful that were personally loyal to Lucio. One of those squires was Keveyn. Keveyn was boisterous, suspicious and self-minded. Kevyn was an avid competitor. The only way to stand up to him was to yourself become ardent. A bosom comrade of his was Timothy. Timothy had the look of a young, innocent child, almost docile. He would look at people with his mouth open and elicit pity. The truth was that he was unrelenting and ruthless. Then there was Franuch, who was visibly mean. He was big. The size and shape of his head was like that of bull. The demeanour and expression on his face let everyone know he was a serious man. Marius was the other notable squire in Lucio's camp. He was slim and quick. Unlike his other colleagues who answered to Lucio, Marius was refined. He was about the same size as Brandyn, polite, shy and very observant. Brandyn thought that he would definitely be someone to watch carefully during the games.

The meals at the castle were bountiful and colourful, splendid affairs. Apart from the odd childish pranks that the squires played on each other, life was for the most part pretty fun and exciting. With the loss of Woodcroft, however, he could only think of how Lord Welledon and Meaghan would feel when they got the news. He longed to go home and see how his family was doing. He did not like that Lucio quickly set out from Mead directly for Galles without delay. Brandyn regretted not going. He should have insisted on going too. He was welcomed as a family member. Brandyn had mixed feelings at the time. He thought about April, a young girl he knew back home. She had just been a friend, but now he longed to see her. Despite the diversions of a squire's life and the excitement, he missed being in the company of the people who loved him. He missed his family and the feeling it gave to be a member.

For now all he wanted to do was return to the Wendover Lowlands to see his family and to be home. He wanted to reflect on what had happened. The recent events happened so fast. April always came to mind, and he welcomed any reason that meant he could go home. It was again the late fall, and the Harvest Moon Fest was only a month away. He had already started the serious training. He assessed himself with needing to build up his skills through practice and to build up and maintain his endurance. Brandyn reasoned that taking a trip home by himself would be just the experience he needed. He could wear the full armour ensemble and ride home. He had never ventured out anywhere alone. He thought he could survive and prove himself capable. He would also be building up his endurance on the trip.

When Lucio returned from Galles, Brandyn asked him about Welledon. Lucio told him that Welledon was upset at not having seen him. It upset Brandyn to hear that. Brandyn would gladly have gone to see Welledon. In fact, Brandyn was looking for Lucio to tell him that he would go to Galles when he learned that he had already departed. Lucio calmed Brandyn down by telling him that he explained to Welledon on his behalf. He did not tell Brandyn what it was that he had said to Welledon though. Lucio just told him that Welledon had understood. Brandyn did not believe him. In reality, when Lucio returned the ring that was on Woodcroft's finger, Welledon was disappointed that it was not Brandyn that presented it to him. He was surprised that his son's squire did not return it to him, as was customary. Welledon did not blame Brandyn; it should have been Lucio who insisted he come. Welledon was hurt by the death of his son and seeing Brandyn would have provided a measure of comfort. Welledon never liked Lucio, but he was made Federics' ward by the will of Graedon and that was that. Welledon did not trust Lucio. Welledon wondered what would become of the people, his castle and lands if he should now die. Would Graedon grant Galles to Lucio?

Lucio was very supportive of the notion that Branydn should return home. He even insisted. Lucio had never insisted that Brandyn accompany him to Galles to return Woodcroft's belongings to Welledon. If he had been better advised, Brandyn would first have accompanied Lucio to Galles to return the ring and the other property to Welledon. Brandyn had been away from home a long time. Under the circumstances, an extra four days to go to Galles and back would not have made any difference. Instead, Lucio discouraged Brandyn from going to Galles but encouraged his return to Wendover. Lucio thought that returning to Wendover was just the thing for Brandyn to do. Lucio reaffirmed his sorrow at the death of Woodcroft. He also reminded Brandon not to stay away too long. Silently, Lucio hoped that he would never return. Outwardly, he welcomed Brandyn to train and practise with his sponsors to the knighthood. Lucio was gracious and compassionate when he spoke.

"I can understand that you need time to reflect on what has happened. The journey home and back should be just the thing. Be sure to greet your parents and sister for me, and come back to us safely. Did you make provisions? I will let the kitchen people prepare food for your journey." At that, Lucio left with a sense of urgency.

On the Road

Lucio appeared accommodating. His true thoughts were that the boy still needed to be "weaned" from his mother. Lucio could not care less if he ever came back. And so Brandyn gathered to himself some provisions for the journey and set out. He was happy, yet sad. Brandyn wanted so much to become a knight, but he had not counted on what happened to Woodcroft. He missed the support and encouragement that Woodcroft gave him. He had learned how to read and with more practice could shape his letters into writing. Woodcroft advised Brandyn like he was his blood brother. That was the reason he should have rode to Galles to see Welledon. He was considered family by him. That was the reason that he felt guilty about not going. Brandyn had broke bread at Welledon's table with Woodcroft. At Woodcroft's death, he did not even as much journey back to return his ring. Here he was though with Woodcroft's armour and horse. He felt like a thief.

He would go back to Galles to see Welledon and tell him of his son's bravery and wisdom in serving the people. He would also apologize for taking his armour and return Vento. For now though, he had a yearning to go home to Wendover. The journey to Wendover would take about four days. The return trip would also take four days. He realized that he had to return on time to compete in the tournament games. He could not wait any longer as the door of opportunity was closing with each passing day. He decided that he would go home first. Such a journey would challenge his survival skills and sharpen his senses. His task would be namely finding enough food and not being food himself for wild animals.

The journey was a challenge as the sun in the early day made the ride uncomfortably hot. The breeze was welcome but sometimes became a strong wind that cast dust in his eyes. The search for food was not always reliable. Fortunately, there were many creeks that ran across his path. Although freshwater was available and abundant, catching fish proved to be frustrating. As quick as he was to capture a fish, its struggle to be free coupled with its slippery skin made it hard to hold on to. At one instance he lost his balance and fell in the water himself. On the next occasion that he grabbed the slippery fish, he did not squeeze it. Instead, he threw it on the grasses by the bank of the stream. He had to be quick to recapture it from the grasses too, as the fish wriggled with purpose to return to the water. He collected a few rocks to make a border for a fire. He gathered dried chunks of wood and some dry grass and built a fire by the stream. The moment that the sun went down, his wet clothes gave him a chill and he had to spend time collecting more fuel for the fire. He managed to dry his clothes, but it was too late to resume travelling on that day. He was also tired. After cooking and eating the fish with the bread he brought, he gathered more fuel. After acquiring ample wood stock for the night, he built up the fire and fell asleep beside it. Vento laid down to rest, but he kept watch.

He awoke early the next day and set out with determination to make up lost time. By the time late morning came around, it looked as though he would get another soaking. This time the weather threatened to rain—and it did. He would now have to get off the road and find shelter in the rocky hills. He was careful to walk his horse over the sharp rocks. Brandyn found an ideal shelter that kept the wind and water out. There he could build a cosy fire if only he could attain dry wood. This time he would have to use the last of the bread he packed for the journey, as hunting or fishing would not be possible. After being unsaddled, Vento was happy with eating the wet grasses. Given that all creatures were taking cover in their homes and shelters, it would be improbable that hunting would yield any positive result. The forest animals were taking cover too.

Unlike the first night when he was fatigued and slept effortlessly, this night Brandyn felt afraid. His dwelling place was hard dirt and rock. The few sticks he gathered to light a fire were damp. When they finally started to burn, they began smelling and smoking. Some smoke got into his eyes and they began to tear. He wiped his eyes on his sleeve. He began to think of all that had happened. He thought how safe he could have been if he had stayed at Braemar Castle. Maybe he should have gone to Galles. In either place he would have food and be in the company of many. He compared these places to his present situation. He was cold, hungry and alone. Vento kept his spirits up just being there. He decided that he just had to go home though. He prayed to God that he might protect him this night. He just yearned to be home.

He prayed to God, the God of St. Zorren. St. Zorren was a brave, young knight of Peregren who delivered the kingdom from a winged serpent. He prayed that God might protect him this night. He wanted so much to be like St. Zorren, who was fearless, brave and true. He remembered a prayer that his mother had taught him. His mother told him to give thanks to the Lord always, not just when you need something. He prayed, "I thank Thee Father in Heaven, You are so good to me. I know that You give me everything I need. Amen."

He repeated this prayer until he fell asleep.

It would rain nearly all night and when it stopped, the warm earth contrasted the cool rains and a heavy fog ensued. The sunlight fleeting through did not help visibility either. At least it was not windy. The better part of that day was humid and chilly. In the stillness there was a silence you could hear. In that moment he remembered to thank God for delivering him safely that night. He was already out of food. He asked God that He straighten his path home. Although you could not see very far, all his senses were keen. Brandyn saddled Vento and led him back to the road. There was an eerie beauty to the scenery around him as he mounted his horse and travelled slowly down the road toward the Wendover Lowlands.

After a good time about the noon hour, the silence was broken by the sound of horses pulling a wagon. As they approached, there were two men hauling what appeared to be vats full of ale. The two men riding had travelled from Mead, a small village about three days ride from Braemar and about two days from Wendover. Mead was famous for their single malt spirits and ale. Brandyn recognized the men from when they traded their ale and spirits to his father's tavern for a supply of special grains. The two men recognized seeing this face before, and when he identified himself as Malcolm's son, they knew who he was. They were well-acquainted with his father, whom they had done business with. Andrew, son of Arthur of Mead, and his cousin, Megenes were famous for their festive brews. They were making the first of many trips to Braemar Castle by royal command with a supply for the upcoming Harvest Moon Fest tournament and games at month's end. That was the very place Brandyn needed to be in order to qualify for knighthood. He was going in the opposite direction.

Since it was time for a meal, the two brewers of Mead invited Brandyn to join them—and he did. Megenes had been acquainted with Brandyn's father. Megenes had often purchased barley and oats from him, and in turn he sold him ale and spirits for his tavern. They had heard of the boy from Wendover who became a squire, never imagining that it was Malcolm's son. Andrew told Brandyn outright that he should have stayed home and helped his father. In his mind, their's was the life. Running about as a soldier would get you killed for nothing. Brandyn immediately thought about what happened to Woodcroft and tried to explain the situation. He conversed with them. "I was asked to be a squire by Woodcroft of Galles. Woodcroft consulted with my father and he approved." He paused briefly as the two men listened. "If I become a knight I will be posted to Wendover when they build a castle there. When that happens, not only will I have an allowance from the king's purse, but I could help my father as well."

The two men looked at each other. Brandyn had explained his intentions clearly, and they were worthy intentions at that. He sincerely meant to serve the Wendover community with fairness. Brandyn, after all, had a vested interest.

"The boy sounds sincere," Arthur relayed to Megenes, as he worked busily to prepare their meal.

"Now that he does," replied Arthur. "That he does."

The two men knew that Brandyn was sincere and meant well, but they thought he was a bit of a dreamer. If you are going to dream about a "castle in the sky," it might as well be at Wendover. The brewers knew that there had been talk about building a castle at Mead too, for years now. Despite the cynicism, this unexpected meeting proved to be inspiring. Brandyn met working people he could relate to from the area that bordered Wendover in the southwest. It was as if he had met up with family. The experience was encouraging, and he was lucky to partake in the meal. Brandyn finished his meal and thanked the two "country cousins" and set out again for home. The rest of Brandyn's journey was met with more agreeable weather, though it did get chilly in the evenings.

The Fields of Gold

The rolling hills covered in golden grain that waved as the wind played through them were a sight all too familiar to Brandyn. The smell of the wet dew on the grains and grass that they would turn into straw was sweet on the senses. He looked across and beheld in the field of barley a familiar figure of a young maiden and her younger sibling. Her hair was as gold as the wheat and swayed freely in the wind. Her face was the most angelic, beautiful face he could imagine. And when she turned to see who was coming, she placed the slender fingers of her hand to her forehead to shade her eyes from the sunlight. She did so, so gracefully that it took Brandyn's breath away. His heart beat louder. As he approached her closer and closer, it made Brandyn yearn for her.

"Look, Father, it's Brandyn come back from Braemar," said April with a voice so soft, it was a miracle that kept Brandyn from falling off his horse. Despite that metal shell, she knew it was him.

"A knight is he now?" replied Cranston, her father. He viewed Brandyn's leaving home an excuse to get out of working his father's fields so he could learn disrespect. The thought was rather sarcastic but Cranston regarded most knights to be pompous peacocks. To Cranston, the knights had become self-centred, self-serving and selective. Under his breath he said of Brandyn, "He looks like one," referring to his armour. "But does he have a title or land or money to back him, so much for these chances to get ahead?"

He was not sure how, but Brandyn pulled himself out of the trance he had been in and managed to greet his old neighbour. "Good day, sir," he said, though his eyes were fixed on April. Cranston did not look up but kept on splitting the wood to stack into cords.

"Seems that they have fed and kept you well. What brings you back to these parts, a new crusade?" he said, as he continued his work.

Brandyn did not gather the sarcasm in his words, so Cranston was justified in his belief that the boy was naive. Brandyn forgot how hungry he was. His thoughts instead were fixed on April. "I am not yet a knight, but I hope to be soon. Woodcroft was killed in battle and now Lucio is sponsoring my quest for knighthood."

Cranston stopped and reflected. "Woodcroft killed? That Woodcroft was an exception. He was wiser than his years."

Cranston remembered Woodcroft's intervention a year earlier that was fair and reasonable. The Wendover region had not heard this news, and in a eulogy-like manner he continued with conviction, "He was a true noble, and his family dealt with people fairly and justly."

Cranston remembered the stories of Welledon and his sons. No neighbour was as brotherly and selfless as the Duke of Galles. Welledon always honored his commitments. Cranston paused from his work momentarily to reflect on the news.

All the while Brandyn looked at April. He realized that he was in love. A wedding that they had attended in Plenitude Church when they were young came to mind. Brandyn was almost four years older than April. She was a little girl, but graceful even then. She was rather quiet and nice to be around. Brandyn remembered that they were secretly married after the formal service. It was merely children at play. While the celebration began outside in the church courtyard and garden, the two young children went back into the church to exchange true love vows. He knew then that he would love no other. It was so innocent, and it did not go unnoticed. The tactful Pastor Mattews was in the vestibule and remained quiet. After he had performed the wedding service, the entire parish followed the newlyweds to the church courtyard and garden. The pastor had run into the vestibule to remove his ceremony robes. He could not help overhearing the two young children and did not want to spoil this precious moment for them. He remained silent through the entire time until Brandyn and April left the altar and went out into the garden as fresh newlyweds. Brandyn remembered how he knew then that he would love no other. Here was the same girl, a young maiden of thirteen years.

Cranston had asked him something. He was not paying attention so he excused himself.

"Have you been home yet?" asked Cranston again.

Brandyn replied, "I have not as yet been home, but afterward would you object to my calling on April, sir?" He paused. "I can assure you I come with noble intentions."

"And which daughter would that be?" he replied, as he continued working as though he could not tell the obvious.

It was rather awkward until Courtenay, the youngest daughter, relieved any tension there was by calling her father's jest. "Oh, Father," she said incredulously in laughter.

Although Brandyn had finally sensed the cynicism, he proceeded carefully, swallowed the lump in his throat and uttered her name, "April." He said so with such gentleness, that there could be no doubt about his intentions.

"We could have him to supper," charged Courtenay, with such enthusiasm as to make Brandyn feel welcome. It was a done deal, as it was suppertime. Cranston was leaning toward asking him to stay for supper, that is why he asked Brandyn if he had been home. Cranston would not refuse a meal to the son of his neighbour and friend. The families knew each other, lived the same lifestyle, faced the same hardships, went to church, and celebrated occasions and holidays too. Brandyn just wondered what Eileen, Cranston's wife, would think about the extra guest at dinner. Brandyn thought that in the meantime, he would just help out Cranston with splitting wood. He could head home after the meal.

Brandyn removed his armour and set it on the saddle of the horse. Courtenay offered to take Vento to the stable and look after him. Courtenay led Vento to the stable, where she removed his saddle and Brandyn's armour. She gave Vento water, and the horse drank his fill. It was cool in the shaded barn. After rubbing the horse's sweat off with a towel, Courtenay brushed Vento's skin and mane. At the wood pile Brandyn set himself to collecting and stacking the chopped wood, which did not seem like a chore now that April was there.

A Farmer's Life

There would be much timber to cut up for cooking and firewood. Winter was just around the corner and always came sooner than you thought. It always did. The apples and pears in the orchard would have to be picked and stored. The fruit trees would have to be pruned. The wheat, oats and barley would have to be brought to the grist mill to be ground into flour. Ale, cider, wine and single malt spirit would have to be made in preparation for a long winter. Everyone boasted about how good their own brew was, but the concoction did not work out every time. The finest brewing of ale most consistently was done by Arthur and Megenes of Mead. Brandyn's father, who ran the tavern in Wendover, believed it was the water from the Langden River that flows through Mead. Its source ran from the high mountains behind Mead that acted as a shield and provided Mead with a cascade of water. It had to be the water. The wheat, oats and barley grains were comparable. The brewing of spirits was also specialized, but that did not stop the amateur. The finer spirits came from the Bendire Monastery that was northeast of Braemar Castle. The monks had been distilling for over a hundred years. They baked good bread too. The monks distilled fine spirits that were blended with combinations of the countless different flowers found in the fields and wild forest behind the monastery. King Lyndorn had once remarked about the spirits of

Bendire Monastery, calling them the "thousand flowers." He was describing the spirit's strength as it was used for medicinal purposes.

There had been a new custom in the fall. The burying of surplus cabbages in tarpaulins so they would keep by virtue of the frost that would hit the land. In Wendover it was not certain where this idea came from, but it was rapidly becoming tradition. Each farmer dug a large pit about four feet square and three feet deep. At the last possible minute before the ground froze, the cabbages were cut from their stem and stuffed into sackcloth. The sackcloth was then put into the pit and covered with earth. By early spring the cabbage could be dug out and used as though it was just cut. It was thought that traders at the seaport brought the notion. Not only did goods get exchanged but ideas got exchanged as well. Other chores included stewing tomatoes and peas and storing onions, carrots, celery and parsnips. Of course there was everybody's favourite chore, digging up potatoes for storage. Every farmer had some potatoes. The serious potato growing was done in the Galleysian fields. These tasks had to be done.

One trick Brandyn remembered his grandfather telling him was that you would place an apple or two among the potatoes being stored. The presence of the apple slowed down the sprouting. By springtime the potatoes would sprout anyway and that would be a sure sign that they would be planted soon. The meat and poultry would come from the chickens, ducks and hogs, but they had to be tended as they were livestock. Any fishing and hunting was a welcome addition to every household. And then you were done. It seemed so easy to list and describe all these tasks, but it would occupy all your time with steady work. There was no time to waste, especially when the weather was a factor in your success. The simple farm life kept you on your toes; there was always something to do and most of the time it would not wait.

Brandyn remembered all the responsibilities and how food made its way to the table. The past few years that he spent at court had made him take things for granted. He thought, though, all that work would not be so bad if April was with him. He imagined having a home of their own and children of their own that they could raise. After a good crop, they could settle in for the winter around a cosy fire in the hearth and celebrate with a big feast. Even Cranston would approve of this happy home with all his grandchildren running around. The idea of farming was very attractive at this point. Again, it was so easy to list and describe these tasks.

By the time supper rolled around, Brandyn had earned his meal. During the work period, April brought some apples and water to her father and Brandyn for them to take a pause in work. The apples were fresh, crisp, sweet and juicy. The last apple that Brandyn ate was last Christmas. It was soft and mushy. Branydn was so hungry he ate two. Since he was not used to stacking wood properly so that it would not fall over, Cranston had to make adjustments to the woodpile. *So much for the help*, thought Cranston. Despite his lack of finesse, Cranston let him take a turn at splitting the wood with the big axe. Brandyn got it stuck in the wood a few times before he listened to his teacher as opposed to trying to show off to April. Because he was not familiar with this work, his hands developed blisters and they broke. Cranston thought it was funny. Brandyn realised it was evidence that he had worked hard to help. April felt proud of Brandyn; she had missed him as well. The more practical Cranston judged by accomplishments. He had planned on finishing before supper. Now with the added help, he would not get done at all. Cranston realized it took patience to show people how to do things, but he knew Brandyn had good will. Good will eventually leads you to success because you actually want to succeed. He did tell him to "mind the stacking" as they switched jobs again.

"Those soldiers and knights make sport of the likes of people like me, your father and the countless others living in small patches all over the place. We scratch in the ground for food so we can feed them," said Cranston, while he was positioning a small log for splitting. “In return,” he paused to swing the axe to the wood, “we get protected.”

Eileen called out that supper was on the table.

While they washed their hands, Brandyn thought about what Cranston had said.

“I see your point, sir, but we have to trust that everyone will do their duty and what is right and fair.”

“You’re still a young boy, much to learn. Your father would tell you no different,” he said, sounding condescendingly.

“I realize that things don’t seem fair sometimes—”

“Sometimes,” the fatigued farmer interjected, “tell me when there is any consideration for the farmer? Does the landlord say, ‘It was a dry summer, you didn’t produce as much, I’ll reduce my taxes’?”

There was much frustration that went with farming. The farmer was the first person to realize he had to feed his brother and the last to get help; even the weather played tricks on him. Eileen, who was busy all day with laundering clothes and had prepared supper, heard enough. She stepped outside and greeted their neighbour’s son. “Glad to see you return, Brandyn. You would think someone might be hungry. The food will get cold.” She looked at Cranston. “The food is hot and ready now.”

Eileen knew that her husband was worried about the harvest. He was tired and she did not want to see him lose his temper and leave a bad impression with Brandyn. She turned to her husband to remind him, “Can you change anything by complaining? It will only steal away what small joy you have with what you got.”

‘But, I was only telling the boy—”Cranston tried to explain but was interrupted. He did not even mention the death of Woodcroft. Cranston did not disapprove of all knights.

“The boy has been brought up straight and true. Why should we be surprised when he speaks of the ideals we all believe could be true? Maybe things will get better with time when the nobles realize that you only need so much to live on. At least we can be grateful that the invasion on Wendover was put down this year." She paused and addressed everyone. "Now let's eat."

Her comments sure made sense. Eileen still planned on preserving the recent batch of cucumbers that evening. She was an industrious woman.

They entered the kitchen. It was the largest room in the house where there was a table set for supper. The table was sure fine; not as fancy as at court, but if you did not count Cranston's abruptness, much more inviting. The family took their place, with Cranston at the head of the table. Brandyn was assigned the seat at Cranston's right and next to April. Seeing that her husband was tired, Eileen said Grace. "We thank Thee Lord for these Thy gifts which we are about to receive. Let them strengthen us to do Your will. Amen."

Everybody repeated "Amen" and supper was about to begin. The food consisted of boiled cabbage with apples and mutton. The bread that Eileen had made was baked on a brick-bottom compartment next to the fireplace. The smell of the baked bread was elating. The bread was so delicious. Eileen had added black currants which softened and spread like a marmalade. You did not have to spread butter on it. Brandyn could have feasted on the bread alone. The meal was so fine and was a pleasure to eat. The hard work earlier seemed to give him an appetite for the supper, that and the fact that April was there. Brandyn made it a practice to eat slowly as Woodcroft had instructed him to do. Not only was eating slowly healthier, but Brandyn could have devoured his meal in an instant. He was hungry from the trip. Now normally they would use water to wash down their food, but with a guest, apple cider and ale were served. It was customary to bring out what you had when a guest was dining. Brandon mixed a little cider with his ale to lighten the drink. April added ale to her cider. Eileen smiled. Cranston kept his thoughts to himself.

To make conversation, Brandyn thought he might introduce the idea of policing Wendover and the king's highway. The responsibility would bring in a wage and he could work the land as well. He should stand a good chance of being sent to Wendover if he could become a knight. The region needed policing and protection from enemy raids. The need to build king's post bridges over the deeper streams had to be overseen. Brandyn believed that the residents of the area could relate to him. Being a resident himself, he knew the deer paths in the forest, the passes in the escarpment and streams. He had often accompanied his father to these places. He would have a vested interest in keeping peace and protecting the people and their lands. Both goals were vital to King Graedon as well. All this would hinge on his success at his up and coming test.

"If you stay long enough to help the community with chores, you shall gain the strength, versatility and reason you need to become a knight," said Cranston. It was the most positive notion that came out of Cranston since he got there, even though it came so late in the evening.

"And after I'm done at home I shall come to lend a hand here," he declared as he glanced at April. "I need all the training I can get, if I am going to gain knighthood."

No one doubted Brandyn's sincerity; they all knew he meant well, even Cranston.

Things were working out just fine. Brandyn knew that he would have to head for home, as it was getting late. Travel after dark was never safe, but at least he knew the roadway well. He thanked Eileen for a fine meal and the company. He thought how the meals in the king's court did not even compare to that table set about the fireplace and these good, kind-hearted people. He did not have to guess at what these people were thinking about, except for Cranston, but he was tired. The tables at court were fully furnished with food and drink, but you were always being watched. Somehow you could not enjoy it. There were many refinements and carefully chosen words and manners that somehow lacked sincerity at court. The meal he had just enjoyed was simple and modest. Keeping up with Cranston was not easy, but at least you knew where you stood with him.

"I had better be on my way," he said as he turned to April.

Brandyn was hoping he could say goodnight to April outside alone, but his chances did not look good. April and Courtenay were already assisting their mother with clean up and dishes. Cranston was tired so he moved to the large chair and sat quietly by the hearth. He sat back and put his feet up against the fireplace. Brandyn thanked Eileen for the fine supper once more. Since Cranston had quickly fallen asleep in his chair by the fireplace, Brandyn quietly bid April and Courtenay a good evening and told them it was fun to be there. He walked to the barn where Vento had been resting in the cool barn. It was now cooler outside since the sun set. It had been a lengthy journey from Braemar Castle. Brandyn was tired as he put on his armour. He knew he would not be hot in it now. He realized that it was Vento who carried him in full armour and his saddle the entire way. Courtenay had done a fine job of brushing his coat and tending to the horse's needs. Brandyn placed the blanket on Vento and then the saddle. When he had finished, he walked the horse outside and was about to mount it when he saw April come out to fetch water to rinse the dinner utensils and plates.

"I'm so glad you came along today," she said. "When you went away it was so sudden."

"I wasn't expecting to see you, but I'm glad I did. April, I thought about you every day. I missed you something awful. It felt as though I would never see you again. I had to return. There isn't any girl as beautiful as you, not even at court."

"Not even the princess?" April questioned. "I've heard that she is beautiful and looking for a husband."

"She's pretty I guess. I have seen her, but I never spoke to her. She doesn't even know I exist. If she loves another it would not bother me."

These words pleased April. Brandyn found himself moving closer and closer to her until he could not make sense of their conversation. He reached for her shoulders and drew her to him, but before he could press his lips to her mouth, her mother called for her and the water.

"April!" she cried. Eileen was waiting for April to return with the water for rinsing so she could start her pickle preserves. "How long does it take to get water?"

"Coming, Mother!" She turned gently to Brandyn. "I've got to go," she said gently as she scurried to get the wooden pail of water to the kitchen. "Good bye."

"I'll see you soon," Brandyn reassured.

He was rather pleased at how well the whole evening went. On the ride home, Brandyn could have kicked himself for not kissing her.

Ill Tidings

As Brandyn approached the lands his father worked, he could see evidence of his father's handiwork. His father could tie the barley and wheat very neatly for transporting but he did not stop there. Even the grasses that would feed the livestock were neatly tied. "If you do something, do it right," he would always say. He could see the light of the fireplace in his home, the Wendover Tavern. At a distance he could identify the silhouette of his sister Meaghan in the dark. Joy overcame him; he was home. When Meaghan saw the armour, she was filled with gladness for she thought it was Wills. She referred to Woodcroft as "Wills." He had come to pay her a visit. She ran to greet the knight. Brandyn rode a little farther and then dismounted the horse. With open arms he greeted his sister, who was happy to see him. Nonetheless, she was surprised at it being Brandyn in Woodcroft's armour. It did not dawn on her that anything was wrong with Woodcroft. After all, he was training Brandyn for knighthood. Perhaps, she thought, he had already made it. Maybe her brother did something so heroic that he was knighted then and there on the battle field.

The matter did, however, dawn on Brandyn, and his sullen expression told Meaghan that there was some troubling news. Brandyn could not find in himself the words to tell his sister about the death of her beloved "Wills." By the look on his face, he did not have to. Meaghan waited patiently and held on to hope. She heard her brother say, "Woodcroft is dead. He was killed in battle. Lucio gave me his horse and armour."

Naturally she gathered, why else would Brandyn have his armour and horse, yet she could not believe it. She did not want to believe it. She much preferred her earlier illusion. Maybe this was not happening. Maybe she was imagining it. She began to breathe deeper and faster. Then Meaghan let out a cry that Brandyn would have done anything to prevent. If only he could have prevented it. So there he stood with his sister hugging the shell of armour around his body like she had never embraced anything before. Tears sprung from his eyes. These were the tears that should have sprung from his eyes when he first observed his lord's slaying. At the time, he was too much in shock to do so. Malcolm and Andrea ran out to greet Brandyn but were stopped in their tracks by the tragic scene before them. Seeing their son in Woodcroft's armour and Meaghan crying in his arms told them everything. Woodcroft was dead.

Reassessment

Malcolm was not so sure about his son's opportunity to gain knighthood. Look at what happened to Woodcroft. Lord Welledon, the great Duke of Galles, Woodcroft's father, had a castle and subjects to govern in Galleysia to the southwest. He had lands, money and a voice at court, but little did that do for either of his sons. Now Brandyn wanted to follow in their footsteps. Perhaps the decision he had made earlier to allow Brandyn to be a squire for Woodcroft was not wise. He did not believe it though. Malcolm knew that their freedom came with a price. Evil would flourish if they allowed it to. If no one stood up against tyranny, it would engulf everyone. It was these brave men, many of them young, who stood up to tyranny and treachery. They were the defenders of freedom.

Earlier Malcolm did not really miss his son's help with work on the farm. He was now a little older. He could use some help from his boy, who was more like a man now. In the end, he had to allow his son to make his own decision. Malcolm never had the opportunity to be a knight, so did it mean that his boy should not have it?

It was a sacrifice. He reasoned, "What was not a sacrifice?"

That is why he let him go in the first place. He wanted his son to have a chance at a better life. Yet, he felt foolish to have sent him away when he could have taught him how to make a living. The opportunity presented itself, so he let him go. Why should he change his mind now?

Malcolm knew how to fight too. The king's men were not always on time to defend the farmers from raids, you know?

Malcolm reaffirmed in himself that he would teach his son all he knew and support Brandyn's quest for knighthood. Convincing Andrea might take some time. It was what his son wanted.

He would teach his son all he knew.

Brandon knew he could not stay away from Braemar Castle for a long period of time. Lucio, he believed, would expect him to train along with his group of sponsors in order to qualify for the contests. In all fairness, it was only right that you train. Can you imagine just showing up on a tournament field and competing without proper instruction and practice?

It was a recipe to get hurt or worse. But just like Cranston suggested, he could be licked into shape by the farmwork. Now that it was harvest time, there was still plenty of farmwork and late harvesting to do. The fact he wanted to see April was a good reason to train at home too. Not that he did not see April; she was all he could think about. He could close his eyes and see her face.

Cranston was certainly capable of defending himself and despite his cynicism would take his part in shaping up Brandyn. Cranston knew that Brandyn was "wet behind the ears," but he also knew he was sincere and showed respect for his elders. These items mattered a great deal to the farming community. Brandyn then would stay at Wendover, work with the elders of his community and train under their guidance and judgment.

Commitment

The sun rose early, and a good thing it did. The day might have started with soaked fields from a rainfall. During the harvest, rain was not desired, as it made it impossible to separate the chaff from the grain. The harvest would be delayed until the crop was dry. The king's share was already collected and shipped. The remaining fields were the farmer's yield. There were several neighbours that had joined them to gather the grain. After a sop of bread in wine and some bacon, they all set out to the fields. Brandyn was enthusiastic about helping, but his inexperience and lack of skill rendered his help not worthwhile. He had never collected barley or tied it into sheaves. There was also the resentment from the other boys about his age who would never be squires. They could easily best him at farm chores. Malcolm was patient, however, with his son. How can you expect the very best from someone who is just beginning the job?

"If you can concentrate on cutting the sheaves, I'll bundle it for a while," suggested his father. Unfortunately, Brandyn was not doing an even job of that either. Malcolm had to show him how to hold the scythe and move it about in even strokes and keep his balance while always moving forward. This was a skill that required not only strength to hold up and swing the scythe, but you had to have good balance. The cutter had to move his body in harmony with each swing that took him back and forth. Upon returning the scythe to Brandyn, he continued in his butchering and at that his father lost patience.

He raised his voice at him. "Slow down and do it as I showed you! Get the feel for it first then you can speed up."

Of course this chastisement was deserved. With all the others doing the cutting like a synchronized ballet, it was clear that this would-be knight lacked poise and coordination. In other words, they would massacre him in the games, let alone in real combat.

Before the first hour went by, Brandyn's hands were broken in callouses and he was tired and discouraged. It was one thing to have been a squire and run errands for Woodcroft, but to keep on track with these repetitious labour tasks, well, he did not care for them. The other farmers were either annoyed or making sport with him. Brandyn realized that to say you are going to do something and actually doing it are two very different things. The men gathered there to collect grain were serious. This was their food to get them through winter. There was no time for training an upstart. Brandyn was turning into a liability. The truth was that it was Brandyn's attitude that was the problem.

When the men came back from the fields, his mother Andrea had set a fine table for their meal. The men had surely earned their keep that day, and tomorrow they would do the same at the Garvyn farm. Brandyn was starved but more tired than starved. He remained rather quiet while all those that gathered there made sport of his shortcomings on the grainfields. The younger boys avoided him with silence. Brandyn excused himself and went outside, where he walked over to the weeping willow tree that leaned over the brook. He lay his back on its thick branch. The sound of the water running over the rocks in the brook was relaxing. The sun had nearly set in the cool evening weather. In the time he spent there he thought about everything. He thought about April and how she would not be so proud with him today. He still clung to the hope that he could win her by becoming a knight. It seemed that farming would be hopeless for him.

By all accounts, the second day, which should have gone better, did not. But he was doing his best, or at least he thought he was.

He questioned himself because in all his plans and dreams, he was celebrating the results. He was going to be a knight, he was going to farm, he would have April for his bride. He had not failed, yet. He had a plan. He just failed to work the plan. At the end of the third day, just when his attitude changed for the better toward this remedial, repetitious work, his father stepped in and gave him a tongue lashing.

"Even if you make ten mistakes today and only nine tomorrow, I would say that you are improving. But you are not. Any squire, let alone a battle lord, could put you down and humiliate you in an instant. In a real battle you would be slain. How badly do you want this quest for knighthood?"

"It is all I have ever dreamed of," he told his father. "Then there is you and the tavern and farm. And whether I am to settle down on a portion of this land and have my own family—"

"Maybe it is time that you focus on one task at a time," interrupted Malcolm.

"You said yourself I should take the chance. When Woodcroft asked you about making me his squire, do you regret me getting the chance?"

"No, just your throwing it away because you do not have the will to see it through. Most of our neighbours think I am a fool to have allowed you to go. While their children learned how to make a living, I sent you out to find a 'better' life. I wonder now if I was right in doing so."

"Not everybody gets this opportunity, Father."

"Then do not squander it!"

Keeping a Commitment

As the day passed, verily Brandyn grew more and more coordinated, bringing out the best in everyone. There were friendly competitions with the other boys. The farming community would not be outdone by an upstart. Slowly, he was winning over acceptance into the group. One of his peers, a young boy named Tomas, asked him about his adventures, duties and any secrets about knighthood. The others listened tentatively as he told them stories about the battles and the king's court. It seemed every young boy had the same dream. They wanted to be a knight and rescue a damsel in distress as well. Brandyn told them, "You yourselves hold the key to knighthood. It is the desire for truth and honour that your hard work and devotion to your family and community has provided. Anyone can attend court and show chivalry by defending the people they love. These qualities it seems you already possess."

With that statement Brandyn had won them over to him. Even the older boys noted that he had respect for them despite their being field workers. Although the trying labour continued, it seemed to be more manageable now that Brandyn was part of the team. It was amazing what a positive attitude could do.

At night when no more work could be done, some mock battles took place with walking sticks, then swords and axes. Mitchell's sons were crafty with the quarter staff, especially Matt, who was a year older than Brandyn and who also took note of April's beauty.

When they were young, Brandyn had fashioned a well-crafted slingshot from oak wood. It was sleek and strong. It even impressed James, the woodcarver in town whom Brandyn was proud to show. Matt was jealous of it. He felt that it was his responsibility to destroy it before Brandyn hurt someone with it. Matt asked Brandyn to see it. When Branydn, all too glad, handed it over to him, he broke it. Matt knew how much time and careful carving it took to make the slingshot. He knew that Brandyn was proud of it and that he would never hit another person. He broke it anyway under the guise of "being his brother's keeper." How considerate. Brandyn made a point of remembering that day every time Matt challenged him with the quarter staff. Brandyn seemed to rise to the occasion.

The trials continued when they got home. The long branch of the weeping willow tree that stretched over the brook served as a test for balance. It was wide and long enough for two combatants to try and knock one another off. The dunk in the cold water was a reminder that you were not swift enough. Malcolm did not hold back on his son. He had to provide real offense so his son could experience what the tournament would be like.

"What you need are lessons in dance. Didn't you observe dancers at court?"asked Malcolm.

"Dancing didn't impress me,"Brandyn replied reluctantly.

"It should have. Think of the pretty maidens that enjoy a good dance. Not only that, but dance allows you to move about gracefully, following direction from the music and developing your coordination so you don't get knocked in the water."

All the while Malcolm was speaking, he was demonstrating the footwork, rhythm and coordination that landed his son in the brook with a wet thud. Malcolm laughed. Although it is not easy being laughed at, Brandyn saw that his father was pleased with his efforts and that he did support him. Malcolm would always support his son. In fact, he believed in his son and knew that Brandyn had good will and the ability to succeed. Andrea even insisted on him learning a few dance steps. In the tavern she danced with him to a tune that she sang. Andrea reasoned that you never know when dancing would come in handy. Of course, Andrea was thinking of the get together the Wendover farming community would celebrate after everyone was finished with the harvest. There were many pretty girls that enjoyed a good dance.

The mock competitions occurred even when they took time to rest from work in the afternoon when the sun was at its peak. After witnessing the youths thrashing that morning, the farmers were surprised that they could still compete. Fenwyck remarked, "You know all is well when they still have strength after this mornings work."

Garvyn answered, "Of course they have strength, Finn. They are young."

The "friendly" rivalry between Matt and Brandyn gave each other enough fuel to compete. So the training continued well into the second week. Although there was not much time to see April, in a few days they would be at Cranston's farm for harvesting.

Vested Interest

When the day to help Cranston arrived, Brandyn made sure he got up early despite the fact that he had trouble falling asleep. It was perhaps because he had planned every speech and action for the entire day. To see April was the only thing on his mind. He, of course, would take the lead when it came to overseeing the chores and making sure things got done proper. This certainly was a good idea to have a plan in mind. It would provide an advantage over the affairs at hand. Since it was the last farm to harvest this year, the entire farming community would come to together to have a meal and get together on the last day. It was Cranston and Eileen's turn to host.

In the field, Brandyn moved lightly on his feet, and when he grabbed something to be stacked, it was getting stacked properly. Things did not clumsily slip out. He worked with purpose, a plan and direction. Malcolm was proud of his son. Although he had started somewhat slowly, he made himself useful. There would be rivalry when it came to the other boys. A certain amount of rivalry is healthy. Each boy wanted to impress his girl. There were several pretty girls from the community getting dinner ready. Later they would be available for the harvest dance to celebrate the end of harvest. By far the most beautiful in Brandyn's mind was April. Brandyn was not the only boy who had designs for April.

At supper Brandyn was courtly, sitting smart, speaking politely and waiting graciously. He ate well-mannered but did not act conceited. He did not treat the others condescendingly. He even offered to assist with getting more water. It seemed all was going well until the dancing started. Brandyn was distracted by the conversation he was having with Courtenay when Matt, one of Mitchell's sons, asked April to dance. It was innocent enough; April could not refuse Matt a dance. Matt was pretty graceful with his feet and cast a fine shadow. Coordination comes to those who work at it. Brandyn was infuriated. This rage would not be apparent except that his eyes opened wider and his jaw was stiff. He had lost his composure and focus. He had never experienced this feeling before. There was a strange heat that overcame him. He felt strong. He felt he could do anything. He could do anything but see April in another man's arms. Courtenay realised Brandyn's distress and rescued him by leading him to the dance area. When Brandyn regained his composure, he was grateful to Courtenay. It seemed April's little sister was wise beyond her years. She too thought that Brandyn and April should be together. Brandyn thought that it sure helps to have the approval of April's little sister.

When the first dance ended, Brandyn wasted no time in walking over to April and asking her for the next dance. If Matt had his way he would have continued to dance with April, but she walked away from him toward Brandyn and her sister. When Brandyn took April's hands and danced with her, he hoped the music would never end. April felt the same way. Brandyn was not pompous and assuming as some other boys she noticed—and he was gentle. She felt safe with him. Brandyn mustered the courage to speak some heartfelt words. "From the moment I saw you, I knew you were the one. I fell in love with you. I cannot imagine what life would be like without you. There is nothing that I cannot do. Nothing that I would not do for you. Nothing, except see you with someone else. I could not bear to see you with someone else."

Anyone could see that these two were in love. Since it got cooler in the evening after sunset, you could see the chill in the people's breath. More wood was added to the fire that was built just outside the barn. The fire was a splendour of colour and warmth. It was the very fire that had roasted the lamb that they ate for supper. The people gathered in their chatting groups around the fire and sat up against the hay, the wooden bench or leaned against the wooden fence. Fresh chestnuts were gathered and shelled. The outer casing had a natural dye that stained the hands of the handler, but it was worth the sweet treat. Unsweetened tea went best with roasted chestnuts, and the hostesses had preheated tea pots and brewed a tea from mint leaves. Apples were pressed in the vat and fresh apple cider was available.

It was at that time that Brandyn and April slipped away from the celebration and stood under a great oak tree near the brook. They were both of them transported to a dream world as they stared in each other's eyes. They did not have to speak. It was cool outside. They did not sense the surroundings except for the sound of the babbling brook and the sweet smell of cut grains. It was these sensations that Brandyn would carry with him. The look of her face was burned into his mind. At that point Brandyn put his hands on April's shoulders and slowly brought her toward him. He pressed his lips to hers firmly and then withdrew them to see April's eyes. April embraced her arms around Brandyn and they kissed again. "Will you marry me?" asked Brandyn.

"Yes," she replied. He wasted no time in kissing her again.

Brandyn would be gone to Braemar Castle for who knows how long. Parents in Wendover did not believe in long courtships, but this was sincere. There was nothing Brandyn could not do now. He would work hard to make his dreams come true so he could be with April. The joy of that moment spent was a part of history. It happened and Brandyn was thrilled about holding the girl of his dreams. April held him right back. It was love true love. He thought that no matter what, no one could change what had just happened—no one.

Return to Braemar

The journey back to Braemar Castle would be effortless. In late September the weather was cool but the sun shone. Unlike the trip he made to get home, Brandyn was confident. He had purpose and direction. April chose him. It was not a dream. She chose him and he held her and kissed her. After bidding goodbye to his parents and sister, he passed by Cranston's farm to see April once more before heading off to Braemar. They took a walk in the fields that were once tall grain but still covered in golden straw cast against the backdrop of blue sky. Neither the grain nor the sky were a match for beauty compared to April's hair and eyes. If that was not enough, April handed him her scarf. This was extremely significant on two counts. First, it was customary that a knight carry the colours of his lady. So Brandyn took the scarf from April and tucked it in his breast. Secondly, it was April's scarf. She did not have a chest full of them; it was her only one. It was his now. They kissed again before he mounted Vento, and he reached down to kiss her once more. Then he rode off. All that he needed to do now was to gain the title of knight, and then he could return to serve Wendover and marry his true love. This was a very simple plan of what he would have to accomplish. He still needed to gain knighthood, and this would prove to be a challenge that would test him harder than anything he had yet encountered.

Contest Day

The day every boy dreams of had come. The games, ceremony and feast that marked the knighting of all squires who were successful in preparing for knighthood and induction in the king's service had finally come. The banners and flags displaying all standards and colours were swinging in the breeze. The sunlit blue sky promised that the crisp autumn morning would rival a fair summer day by noon. A better day, one could not imagine. The field was covered with tents and vendors and entertainers and people and the morning dew.

The people came in celebration of the harvest and to take part in the games and festivities or simply to be entertained. There were wares and food and drink to be bought and consumed among neighbours and friends who had toiled in preparation for the long winter months ahead. Other than farming and survival, there was little amusement. The smoke of the burning wood for food preparation was the only item obstructing the scenery, but with it came the appetizing smell of various flesh including goat, lamb, chicken, goose and pork. With it, the bewitching aroma of apple cider could be sensed, but the smell of fresh baked rolls wore down any resistance.

The young children wasted no time in dividing themselves into two teams and playing football. The game required a suede skin, about the size of a knight's helmet, to be stuffed with a small rock the size of a man's clenched fist that was wrapped in old rags and then stitched with suede strips of twine. Two stakes fashioned from wood from the nearby forest were pounded into the ground opposite each other by one hundred paces. They stood above the ground about four feet. The two teams then used their feet alone to manoeuvre the ball across the field while the players hands were clasped behind their back. The goal was to hit the opponent's peg stake with the ball. When the younger children played, they did not have to clasp their hands behind their back. There were no boundaries or limit to the number of players, or a time limit attached to the game. This activity entertained the youth until the sun set. Often there were disagreements as to the score, as no official kept score.

In no time, more and more children gathered there to play. A group of older adolescents jumped in and took over control of the ball. Another rival group of older boys joined in and the play became too rough for the younger children. The skill and quality of play of the younger boys frustrated the older ones. Finally one of the older boys pushed a younger one off the ball. The bully was immediately rushed by the mass of younger children who had quite enough of the older boys' intrusion. In bringing the bully down, the ball was knocked away and another bully picked up the ball and ran off with it. That practice was definitely against the rules of the game. When the young children surrounded him, the older boy tossed the ball to his colleague in an effort to keep possession of the ball away from the youths. It was clearly against the rules of football to pick up the pigskin or direct it with your hands. The boy was minding the children as he ran with the ball but was not paying attention to where he was headed. He ran right into a woodsman who took hold of him and scolded him for not minding the young children. His friends had run off and the woodsman let him go. The woodsman was the young children's hero as he returned the ball to them. The children continued to play. The only activity that would steal them away from football was the joust, but that would be in the afternoon.

The highlight of the games was the joust in the centre of the tournament grounds. A preliminary event known as the mock joust was very entertaining as well. A squire would have to mount his horse in full armour in a single leap. He would be given a wooden lance with a rounded tip. It was not the same kind they used in battle. Then the squire would try to stay on his horse while the other mounted squires attempted to knock him off his horse. This was to mark the best of the best: very prestigious. The mock joust would take place just before noon so that the squires would be well rested for the afternoon joust.

Dedication

Brandyn thought he would dedicate his becoming a knight in honour of Woodcroft. The example that Woodcroft set for a knight was exemplary. Brandyn was not far from the contest grounds. Before he continued on to the tournament grounds, he dismounted his horse in a quiet place. He looked around to see that he was alone. He offered a silent prayer to God. He knelt by a large moss covered stone and thought, "My Lord and God, grant that I may be safe while in Your service. Grant me Your wisdom and the power to move me to the point of action. Never let me be unfair or unjust or cruel, but let me always serve the truth with honour and dignity. Protect my father and mother and mend Meghan's broken heart. I also pray that Welledon may be comforted at the loss of his son, for I know he is with You now. In honour of Your great knight whom I served, let me compete bravely, and if You deem right, let me gain knighthood in honour of Woodcroft of Galles. He was a true knight and servant of justice and truth. Remember him, O Lord, for we will never forget his good name or deeds. I ask for these things in Christ's name, Amen."

After praying he mounted his horse and rode for the tournament grounds. He also realized that he would see Welledon and he would have to confront him about his son.

There were nine squires hoping to become knights this year and Lucio had in some way influenced every one of them. But today, before the widowed king and his daughter, the young princess, the most true would emerge victorious. There were numerous games of skill that the spectators could enter to win a purse and have bragging rights for a year. There was a log toss and stone throw that excited the spectators as much as the jousting did the squires. Then there was the archery contest and test of swordsmanship, not to mention the food and pageantry.

Spectator's Choice

In the main grandstand the nobility and court of the king were assured their places which overlooked the mainstay of the games—the joust. The log and plank stadium had faded. The paints, too, had faded and peeled. However, not only was the spectacle decorated by banners, ribbons and flags, but the presence of ladies and young maidens. Their gowns added colour, beauty and pageantry, not to mention a gracefulness to the whole affair.

People had gathered there steadily since the break of the sun early in the morning. The vendors arrived even days before. They sought to assure themselves an advantageous place to sell their wares from or secure their supplies and prepare for the important opportunity to make money. There were minstrels to make music and marionette shows. The families, children and youths had eagerly awaited this day for weeks, literally counting down the days and hours. In the last hour the field took shape with everyone who was going to make an appearance—everyone save Brandyn.

The squires under Lucio's guidance gathered together with high anticipation. This was the day they had dreamed about, worked for, agonized over: their only purpose. Lucio had given explicit instructions as to his expectations. He wanted his favourite chosen squires to win. This would have a positive result when it came to influencing the crowds. And, after all, it is reasoned that a good pupil must have had a good teacher. All this would be a positive reflection on him.

When the trumpets belted a crisp arousal, everyone knew the royal party had arrived and that very soon the games would be declared officially started. His Majesty King Graedon was accompanied by his daughter, the Princess Elayne. The princess was escorted on Graedon's arm followed by ministers, counsellors and men of influence, accompanied by their mistresses. They all took their place at the centre of the main grandstand. The people focussed all their attention on their governors. The fanfare was about to begin.

The arrival of His Majesty King Graedon and Her Royal Highness the Princess Elayne signalled that the games were about to begin. King Graedon had been ill and had not accompanied his army to Mead that late summer. Instead he had sent Lucio with the force from Braemar to reinforce the forces of Woodcroft, Dane and Shirewynn. Regardless of his health, there was no way that he would not attend the fall Harvest Moon Fest games. Everyone arose if they were not already standing. A blast of horns silenced the crowds and marked their entrance. They took their place in the royal box at the centre of the grandstand where the nobles and their ladies had attentively waited. Lucio bowed before the king, who proceeded to his chair. Graedon extended his hand to escort the princess to her place beside him. Elayne was accompanied by her aunt, the Duchess Martha, who was Lord Barton's wife, and her cousin Bethany. Other cousins and ladies of the court followed them into their places. Cardinal Spehars took his place amongst the nobles and sat beside Lord Barton, who was the king's high advisor. Federics of Peregren, who had served under Barton, was proud to be there as both Graedon and Barton had pronounced him Duke of Peregren. Although King Jonquis and Queen Enyja of Craigroyston could not attend, they sent Tonio, their envoy. Arno, the envoy of King Henrickard of Leems, also attended. Another notable visitor was Duke Argellor of the Isle of Irminia, whose nephew, Jeremy, was competing in the tournament at swords that day. Duke Welledon was present and caught the eye of Brandyn. Brandyn knew he would have to speak to him about the tragedy of his son, especially since he now wore Woodcroft's armour and possessed his horse and weapons.

Furich, the king's spokesman, turned and faced the field that was now covered with subjects and spoke.

"Distinguished guests, ladies and gentleman! On behalf of his Royal Majesty King Graedon of Rothaynen, welcome to this royal tournament that marks the end of the harvest gathering. His Majesty wishes to thank you, his loyal subjects, for your contributions to our common goal of the betterment of all people and in our quest for opportunity and justice for all."

Furich was referring to the taxes that were recently collected for the king's council to administer for the benefit of all the people. These words were received with reasonable support from the crowd and Furich then turned to the squires there gathered and continued.

"Just like the farmer has ploughed and planted, has pruned and pared and anticipated good results in autumn, so to have these future defenders of the faith, our king and our kingdom also prepared for the rite of passage to the service of God, king and country. And in the presence of God, king and country, they shall compete today in tournament events to prove their worth and determine their place in the eyes of God. To all challengers in the field, fare well and may the best of you be victorious."

There was some cheering, but it picked up as the king himself arose to speak.

"A good day to you loyal subjects of the Rothaynen." Graedon started coughing but regained his composure. "You come from near and far from your castles, villages and steads to celebrate this day of pageantry and games of skill, strength and excellence. We are honored to be joined by our neighbours that have come to observe the games and some to compete as well. May you all enjoy this spectacle, which our Lord God has allowed us the privilege of attending."

The crowds let out a great roar.

Graedon ended with, "And now, let the games begin!"

The crowds cheered louder and returned to being noisy.

The Games Begin

A loud voice in the back announced the hammer throw and started a migration of a portion of the crowd to the south side of the field. Another voice called for the archers to go to their qualifying round for the prestigious silver arrow. The stone throw, where a fourteen-pound stone was hurled, first for distance and then for accuracy, was called to its respective area. Migrations of people followed them respectively. The squires eagerly awaited the light lance and sword competition. In these preliminary events, the idea was to reduce the number of contestants. Eventually the number of contestants dwindled so that the very best could then compete before the main grandstand for a purse, keg of beer, a fine hunting knife or some other premium token. The competitors, friends and family of the competitors all gathered to their respective areas to participate, support and cheer. Others were there to see who was signing on to compete. Some spectators would watch and merely gauge the performance to see if they should have joined. The excitement was contagious. Everyone had a reason to rejoice, eat and celebrate or just get away from the work and enjoy the fanfare for a couple of days.

Lucio was reflective and looked over the grounds.

Keveyn, one of Lucio's squires, noted, "The stone throw competition is nearly over and there is no sign of him."

"By the time he returned to those peasants in that ridiculous suit of armour, they would chastise him. They would put him to work shovelling manure in their barns. He would have no time to train let alone return," uttered Lucio with confidence. "Let us just say that he has returned to his lot in life," Lucio gloated. "The plan worked like a charm."

Lucio felt a satisfaction that everything was going his way. His confidence was unshakeable.

The noise of the festivities was getting louder and muffled the pounding of Vento's hooves. Brandyn now entered the tournament grounds to see and smell the pageantry up close. The journey was tiring but he was filled with enthusiasm. He took out the cloth scarf that April gave him from his breast. It aroused his senses when he brought it to his cheek. With this newly found inspiration, he could do anything. On the other hand, Vento, would need a rest before the joust. The contest of swordsmanship would take place before noon. It was a good thing that the joust was slated for the afternoon—there was just enough time for Vento to rest.

At seeing Brandyn return, the look on Lucio's face was priceless. Disgust, disbelief and displeasure, all rolled into one. His face was a statue. His eyes were fixed in observation. Yet his control and resolve never wavered. Today there was nothing or no one that could challenge let alone change the outcome of his plans. Despite this he was hurt and offended by Brandyn's return—he was not supposed to. It did not please him, but his resolve let his chosen squires know that nothing would spoil his plans on this day.

A farrier approached as Brandyn was dismounting off of Vento.

"A fine animal you have. You plan on jousting today, do you?"

"Yes."

"He will need tending. Bring him along, sir."

"What do you charge? I may not be able to pay you much, but if the money is short I will gladly do a chore for you if that would be alright."

"If you have to ask…" he mumbled under his breath. "So you are not one of them after all."

"Rich, you mean?" Brandyn realized that he had been mistaken for a wealthy squire. It was because he rode in on Vento. "No," Brandyn said in earnest, "I am from the Wendover Lowlands."

The man was disappointed in what he had perceived to be a chance to make good money from a wealthy squire. At that he said something else under his breath and then he went away. Perhaps he repeated, "If you have to ask," and then he went away.

Another colleague of the farrier, who had observed what had taken place between them and thought it to be funny, spoke out, "You cannot blame him; we all need the work. He must have thought that with that armour you have and the fine horse, that he might earn his keep today."

"These belonged to my sponsor, Woodcroft of Galles."

"My name is Tom," said the farrier.

"Brandyn."

"You lack the arrogance that most of the conceited nobles have. Your offer, it sounds fine to me. Come along. Today we get to see who will be 'meting justice in the land.'"

Tom made the last comment in sport. Over the years those who were knighted were not necessarily the best competitors but those who could afford to be there. Many people had lost faith in the manner in which they were policed. Justice was influenced by money and might.

The Swords

Since the contest of swords was going to take place soon, Brandyn left Vento with Tom, while he took Woodcroft's sword and made his way to the grounds where the contest would take place. When he arrived he was greeted by some of the squires he had seen service with. They were glad to see him, but a few select were not. Keveyn, who was Lucio's protege, did not approve of Brandyn since he learned it was not his master's wish that he become a knight.

The swords competition was an important event because after good horsemanship and handling of a lance, a good knight needed to be skilled with a sword. The field was dotted with the candidates paired off to determine who would be eliminated before the final matches. Competitors included entries from all over the kingdom and other lands and not just limited to squires. There were many skilled fighting men and farmers who gained their experience while defending their lands from trespassers. So the squires would have their work cut out for them.

The crowds observed the event from the grandstand seats, the log bridges and the standing room before them. There were tents at the ends of the main field bearing colourful flags. The tents were rented to the wealthier gentry in the event that it rained. The tents were ideal if there was a wind or to keep the sun out of their eyes. The food and drink and comfort that came from watching the competitors, made the spectators feel as if they were in the combat without the risk. The cheers and jeers and instant commentary made it a noisy event. On the field, however, the contestants had only one thought; they were focussed on their immediate opponent. Here tenacity and size mattered as much as skill did. The stronger swordsman could deliver heavier swipes with their blades, but a quick strategian could even the contest if those heavy swipes missed and tired out the opponent. If one opponent hesitated, he lost. You had to be focussed. You could not watch the sport, that was the spectators task. He who watched came in second, not impressive in a contest of two.

Brandyn was ready and fearless; it was the effect that April had on him. He felt that he could accomplish anything. Brandyn's perfomance meant a lot to his father and mother and Wendover in general. There was something larger here. Could this common boy change his destiny?

This contest was a mere stepping stone to the greater scheme of things, so he concentrated on it alone. By the end of the round there were ten contenders left. Among them were three of Lucio's well-trained sponsors, a few farmers, an outlander and Brandyn.

Marius of Marmora was pitted against Jeremy, the outlander from Irminia, a small island northwest of the kingdom that traded with the farmers and merchants at Teresforte. Jeremy was a twenty-two-year-old boatman of fair complexion and long blond hair. His movements were graceful and his manners courtly. Marius put him to the full test and either of them were worthy of the win. Although there was no major score against either opponent, it was Jeremy who was judged to have won. That was the impression of the judges. The contest had been exciting from the beginning to the end. Both contestants were gracious and sportive. Keveyn, Lucio's pride and joy, fought and quickly subdued a farmer's son who could not withstand the fierceness and relentless speed of his strokes. When Brandyn fought John, a local farmer's son, the contest took longer, but it was more of a courtly ordeal. Brandyn managed to win, but he did not hurt John before his home crowd. Franuch, another squire sponsored by Lucio, won in a more determined fashion. On they fought until there were five competitors left.

In drawing lots, Brandyn was to face Jeremy in the next level. Their duel proved to be as fine a display of footwork and skill for the day as Marius' and Jeremy's match. The two were well-focussed and treated the event with the spirit of brotherhood, sportsmanship and concern for the safety of each other. The onlookers appreciated their efforts by cheering and encouraging them both. At one point Jeremy's sword scratched Brandyn's left hand and he relented until Brandyn regained his composure. In a real battle, Jeremy would not relent. There would be no mercy. If it had been a battle, Brandyn could have at one instance sliced at Jeremy's face, but this was a contest for courtly exhibition in as much as for competition. The skill displayed by both actually made each other's performance shine. This was how it was meant to be. In the end though, Jeremy won out with the scratching of his opponent's hand. Brandyn congratulated Jeremy who told him, "If your hand was not stretched out so far, I could never have touched it. When you practise, hold on to your trousers with your left hand."

"What about balance?"

"If you can keep your balance while holding onto your trousers when fighting with a sword, you can do anything."

"Where did you learn that?" asked Brandyn.

"Sailing on a wave-tossed boat," he replied with a smile.

Apart from Jeremy's demeanor, the friendly chat was something that Brandyn would remember. In turn, Brandyn gave Jeremy some advice. "Be careful against these next two, and God's speed."

Jeremy replied, "I gather."

He had sensed a certain childish ruthlessness in the remaining opponents.

Keveyn had observed the contest between Brandyn and Jeremy with great interest. He was surprised at the level of skill that Brandyn displayed, but he now knew what to expect from Jeremy. He thought that no doubt he would eventually face Jeremy. Franuch won his contest, but not as easily as he thought. It was hard fought. He had to charge in with his shoulder and knock his opponent off stride before slashing at his leg for the win. This particular duel was not a crowd pleaser, but it left Keveyn, Franuch and Jeremy to decide the champion of swords. The three drew straws to determine by lot who would face whom. It was Franuch and Jeremy to go first. The winner of the match to face Keveyn. Lucio had placed two squires in the top three but that was not enough. Despite a brilliant exhibition, he was still scornful and unforgiving toward Marius.

The contest between Franuch and Jeremy was fierce to say the least, but Jeremy had been in real combat on his boat. In fighting pirates on the high seas, you do not get another chance if you fail. So as Franuch got fierce, Jeremy too answered in the same fashion, only with grace. Since the affair was a contest and he was a guest in Rothaynen, Jeremy did not employ the killer instinct that he would save for a real battle. Franuch was fatigued but pressed on in anger. In frustration he tried to punch Jeremy with his free hand. With that move committing his body in one direction, Jeremy manoeuvred around and struck his breast plate, scoring the victory. The crowd was pleased to see Jeremy victorious as the truest should win, in the eyes of God. Keveyn had studied it all.

After a brief break that allowed Jeremy to rest, the final contest to determine the best at swords was to begin. Lucio looked at Keveyn and that is all he needed to do to communicate his will. Keveyn was well rested, as he had not fought in this entire final round. Such was his advantage from drawing lots. However, would that rest time away from the competition make a positive difference, or would it work against him?

Keveyn approached Jeremy in the same manner that Brandyn did and bid him good luck. When the challenge started, Keveyn even portrayed himself in the spirit of good sportsmanship. The combatants blades made graceful, skillful moves that lent themselves to a fine exhibit. Just like the previous match between Brandyn and Jeremy, the crowd was pleased with the exhibition and they watched with anticipation. After making the finer moves, the combatants seemed to break for the viewers' judgment. It was like an unwritten law. The spectators approved. This continued for some time. Suddenly, just when Keveyn had left no doubt about his fair sense of play, he smiled and seemed to look away and then caught Jeremy on the chin with his right hand. He then proceeded to take swipes at Jeremy, who valiantly made an attempt to recover and defend himself against the sword strokes. A moment later, Keveyn struck Jeremy's helmet. It was a humiliating way to end a contest for anyone, but imagine for one who had fought so fair and true. There were some cheers in the crowd. There are always cheers when a contestant emerges victorious. In this case, though, there was for the most part ghastly protest denouncing the manner in which the contest was decided.

There was much murmuring that came from the crowd. Lucio glanced over at the announcer, who promptly restored order by declaring the winner of the event. "After a hard-fought contest in which both contestants have distinguished themselves nobly. Let us have a round of applause for these two contestants!" There was applause.

"The winner of the swords event is Keveyn of Strychart."

There was ample cheering, after all it was quite a spectacle and the king was there too. In the end, everyone loves a winner.

Naturally, the food and drink made the tournament games all worthwhile. When the announcer stated "Jeremy of Irminia," however, there was more applause and cheering for him than for Keveyn. Brandyn had immediately rushed out to see if Jeremy needed help leaving the field. He was concerned about the heavy blow Jeremy received to the head. Jeremy's uncle, Argellor, who accompanied him to the games, was present and beheld the whole thing. As a guest in this kingdom, he was not pleased with the treatment of his nephew. Jeremy regained his composure and noticed Brandyn standing there. “Don’t say it,” he directed at Brandyn. “No matter how good you are, there is always somebody better.” Jeremy showed that he was a good sport despite the sequence of actions leading to his defeat. He demonstrated good sportsmanship and had a great attitude with regards to tournament competition. All good competitors subscribed to the notion, “When competing try to win but know that you may lose.”

“He was not better,” Brandyn stated with conviction. “Glad to see you are all right after that blow to the head.”

Brandyn and Jeremy had a built-in rapport from that moment on.

The Ring with the Seal of Galles

Brandyn turned his head and there was Welledon and Argellor walking toward the two of them. Argellor left his guest seat on the grandstand to examine his nephew. Welledon walked toward Brandyn until they were face to face. Brandyn stood toe to toe with the great man. Welledon embraced Brandyn as though it was his own son. A tear came to his old eyes. As Brandyn was about to speak and explain about the armour and horse and sword, Welledon handed him Woodcroft's ring with the seal of Galles. "They forgot to give you this," was all Welledon could say. Lucio had removed the ring from the lifeless body of Woodcroft and returned it to Welledon with his explanation about what had happened. Who knows what story Lucio told him about giving the armour, weapons and horse to Brandyn?

It did not matter because Welledon recognized worth and nobility in Brandyn. The manner in which Brandyn competed to that point in the tournament spoke volumes of his nobillity. Lucio would have killed for the ring with the Seal of Galles. Lucio had hoped that when he returned Woodcroft's ring to Welledon personally, that the gesture would build him a rapport with Welledon. With Welledon's pain at the loss of his son, Luico could present himself as a worthy alternative to Woodcroft. Lucio believed that if anything happened to Welledon, convincing Graedon to give him Galles would be easy.

Welledon was not so easily fooled. He sensed conceit and a certain evil associated with Lucio.

Welledon gave his ring with his family's seal and sovereignty over Galles to Brandyn. Welledon hoped that Brandyn would return with him to Galles. He knew that his son had chosen a fine young man to be his squire. Welledon believed that he would make a fine duke one day. The captains of Welledon's army were loyal and worthy but were growing older in years. These knights had homesteads of their own and were content with their portion of happiness. Welledon believed that he had enough time to groom Brandyn into the heir of his dukedom. Brandyn had been like a brother to Woodcroft. Woodcroft even fell in love with his sister, Meaghan. During the brief visits to Galles, Brandyn had become like a son to him.

Welledon took note that Brandyn had a lady's scarf up his sleeve and realized the boy was now becoming a man. He knew that Brandyn would make his own decisions. Possessing the ring with the seal of Galles was the same as being declared Welledon's heir: a knight no less. "We will sit at the king's banquet tonight and talk some more," he told Brandyn. There were still more events to come, so Welledon turned to Argellor and urged him to return with him to his place among the royal guests.

The Silver Arrow

The focus turned to the archers gallery where the archery competition was to be held. Brandyn did not enter archery because he had not trained. Unlike Lucio's sponsors who were trained at the castle, Brandyn lacked the essential skills with a bow that the average bowman possessed. Without proper preparation and effort, how could you even hope to win against seasoned huntsmen? This was not poor attitude. Rather, it was being realistic and honest with himself. Since he was not properly prepared, he did not enter that competition.

In the end it was the local huntsman who had the final say in the archery event. It was not that strange to see hunters, who made their living by hunting, take the top spots and the "silver arrow" for archery. Marius made it to the top ten before being defeated by more accurate and experienced hands. Marius was a well-rounded competitor in that he had above-average skill in every event. This was inconsequential to Lucio, who was disappointed with Marius' performance that day and with Marius in general. Lucio had passed judgment on him and it was not good. Because Marius did not win, Lucio concluded that he had lost. Brandyn to that point did not compete in as many events as Marius and yet Marius was perceived to have lost.

Test of Mettle

Finally the time had come for the mock joust. With a look to Keveyn and Franuch, Lucio dictated what he wanted. There was no way the contest would be fair. It seemed the selections were already made. The spectators would just have to wait for the results. As for the contest, the odd bruise that accompanied a good wallop was anticipated. However, the squires whom Lucio deemed unworthy would get hurt and hurt bad, accidentally. The majority of the boys were in earnest of doing things fairly and justly, just like the code of good sportsmanship dictated. Since Lucio could count on his sponsors following his wishes to the letter, Lucio arranged for his chosen group to work together. If this collaboration was obvious it would disgrace the squires and even prevent their passage into knighthood. When you have influence over the judges though, it is not that much of a risk. So, organized and in league with a common goal, how could Lucio's chosen lose?

There was to be no teamwork. The contest was to see who could stay on his steed to the end while knocking off the others. Each squire had a blunted wooden lance. Each squire was to engage another with the goal of unhorsing him. There would be no striking another competitor's horse; that would disqualify the offender. Each squire was to defend himself to the best of his ability and in turn try to unhorse his offender. This was, after all, just the mock joust, a tournament game to demonstrate the prowess and the capability of those to whom the responsibility of protecting the land and defending the kingdom of its foes would fall on.

This preselecting illustrated that a handful of people with a common goal can swing the tide in their favor. Lucio wanted to give the people something they had not seen before!

It was as if there was an enemy amongst them. The Duchess Martha, Lord Baron's wife, noted early how a specific handful of contestants had no regard for their brothers' safety. She could only point to them or describe their attire, as she did not know their names.

Oddly enough, Brandyn remembered playing "king of the castle" as a child. When the snow covered the hills on the Wendover Lowlands, it was a favorite pastime. The mountain of snow made it tempting for young boys and young girls to climb up and claim, "I am the king of the castle and you are the dirty rascal." Of course anyone would rather be a king than a rogue, so a challenger would climb up and try to knock the "king" off the hill. Then the new "king" would make the same claim and try to stay on while others tried to push them off. Despite the odd bruise, it was a lot of fun. There was always the odd bully. He or she might use his or her strength and push a younger child too hard. All in all, many winter hours passed with this physical activity. It did not take long for Brandyn to realize it would be exactly the same thing, only more ardent because there were more bullies and the prize was knighthood. Unknown to him was that these bullies were in league.

There was a total of eleven squires in this competition. A few of them were already mounted on their horse and swinging their wooden lance in an effort to prepare for the contest. Keveyn, Timothy and Franuch, Lucio's preferred, stood shoulder to shoulder on the tournament grounds. Their stance communicated that it was their field and the presence of anyone else meant that they were mere guests. They stood there firmly in observance as they watched the others mount their horses, take their lances in hand and enter the field, their field. Since most of the competitors had entered the field, they decided it was time to mount. Keveyn uttered a few words to them and the others nodded. They dispersed and mounted their horses.

Lucio had provided pages to assist the competing squires. They were especially enthusiastic about handing a lance to Keveyn, Timothy and Franuch. That trio were already familiar in the strengths and weaknesses of the other squires from the practice sessions that had taken place at Braemar Castle. These squires were familiar with every other squire's style. They even talked about the others after daily training. They knew all the other squire's moves, all except for Brandyn, who had returned to Wendover. At this point, however, they each agreed with the notion "what could Brandyn do?"

Tom, the farrier, bid Brandyn "God's Speed" and with Vento rested up and groomed, it would be his horse sense that saved the day. The squires that remained at Braemar got ample practice at the joust. In the case of Brandyn, it would be "baptism by fire." At first Brandyn wanted to sum up the field, so he employed evasive manoeuvres in an effort to avoid any blows. Despite that, Randolph, a colleague from Thamden in the Peregren region, caught Brandyn on his left arm that held Vento's reins. The blow was significant at weakening the control Brandyn had over his arm. It also affected the maneuvering of the lance in his other hand. In fact, for a moment he could not feel his arm. He knew he still had the rein in his hand because he saw it there. Brandyn's hand had gone numb. With Vento's experience in battle, the wise steed instinctively took charge over the path his master would take. Vento manouevred the young master out of harm's way until the noble steed sensed that Brandyn regained the control in his hand.

Since Randolph stood out with his assault in that challenge, Keveyn, Timothy and Franuch, Lucio's elite, chose to cut him from the herd. To begin, Timothy rode into Randolph, making it look like he was avoiding some other advance. The collision threw off Randoph's timing as he tried to regain his place on the saddle. Keveyn and Franuch approached, seeming to be engaged in combat but all the while delivering their assaults on Randolph. Keveyn landed a blow across Randolph's face. In response, Franuch added another to his back. Timothy landed his elbow against Randolph's head as he fought to sit up. Randolph was unhorsed to both cheers and jeers from the crowd.

Keveyn became aware of the crowd. He thought quickly. To make it look good, Keveyn took a swipe at Timothy as he was riding by. However, he missed, just as he had planned to. The rest of the action on the field was riveting. Slowly but surely the field was narrowing. Though Keveyn missed Timothy, Brandyn did not. He had recovered from the numbness in his arm and was in perfect position for a swipe at Timothy. Timothy was certain that Keveyn's lunge would miss but he had not calculated on Brandyn being in position. With a single blow Brandyn unhorsed Timothy, who lay in shock and anger on the ground. Timothy made quite a protest and leashed out with words and gestures. Some soldiers had to come and remove him from the field, as it looked like he would attack on foot. Keveyn was livid. He thought Brandyn had taken unfair advantage. It was like "the kettle calling the pot black," so to speak.

In the instant that Keveyn was clenching his teeth, another squire landed a blow to his arm, but with an immediate reaction and great force he returned it. He caught the squire by surprise and knocked him off his horse. Franuch had swung at Brandyn, but Vento stepped back to avoid his master getting struck. With Franuch committed to his lunge, Vento retraced his step forward and positioned Brandyn close enough for him to strike. He struck true, but the stocky Franuch weathered the blow easily. In the process he became angrier.

In the meanwhile, Keveyn planned to attack Brandyn but was forced to defend an attack from another competitor. The battle continued until there were five competitors left. Skill and agility were important but so was endurance. The field was narrowing but mostly due to exhaustion. The weight of the armor, the twists and turns, the balancing act, and handling the long wooden lance were tiring the young squires. The sun had warmed up the previously crisp morning. The sweat inside the armor and on their faces acted as a weight as well. Franuch rode into a squire, forcing him to turn back. Keveyn walloped this weary squire, who fell to the ground like a sack of dirt. Brandyn had subdued another, now leaving Keveyn, Franuch and Brandyn. It was every man for himself now with all eyes focussed on the three.

The contest did not continue though. At Lucio's bidding, Furich used his eloquence at calming down a disgruntled crowd of spectators when he called the contest a draw. Furich asked the crowd to give the competitors recognition for their efforts and for the fine show of skill and endurance. In the presence of His Majesty King Graedon the crowd relented from complaint as the applause drowned the murmurs. Lucio's plan was to have this contest declared a draw, citing the squires' safety and because the formal joust would give them ample opportunity to decide the best. At this point, Lucio wisely decided to call it a draw. He knew that in their zeal and anger, Keveyn and Franuch would double team Brandyn. It would look too obvious and then his own squires would be disqualified. Although Brandyn had been impressive, surprising even Lucio, he had not been outstanding with a decisive first place finish in any event. Since both Keveyn and Franuch finished ahead of Brandyn in archery and swords, all that was needed was a good showing for his boys in the formal joust and his sponsors would receive first honors. The mission would be accomplished. Naturally, this would be a positive reflection on Lucio. The judges tallied the scores.

Knight, Lance and Charger

In the formal joust, a squire was required first and foremost to mount to the croup of his horse in full armor in a single leap. If you could not do that, the quest for knighthood was over. It meant that you lacked the physical conditioning that related tasks required. If successful on the mount, the combatants would then challenge a pre-selected group of knights. Some of these knights were squires as recent as the previous year. The contesting squire would ride his horse across the tournament field and tap the shield that was affixed outside the knights tent. This symbolized a challenge, and the squire and knight would joust until one or the other was unhorsed or the judges ruled a tie.

Since the field of competitors narrowed to five squires, straws were drawn, and by this means it was decided that Marius of Marmora would start off the joust event. Marius mounted his horse and a page handed him a lance. He rode around the field to the knights' tents. He tapped the shield of a knight that was fixed to a pole outside his tent. The knight that he chose to challenge was Lennard of Hilroy. Although Lennard was an older knight, he was quite skilled and quite experienced. Lennard would not, however, take advantage of the squires by bringing harm to them. After tapping his opponent's shield, Marius then rode his horse to the center of the field in front of the grandstand before the King and judging committee. It was not very long before Lennard came out of his tent. He mounted his horse. As his squire handed him his helmet with ceremonial plume, he affixed it on his head. He then took his lance in hand and rode over and joined Marius before the judging committee. Lennard adjusted his visor and hailed the king in respect.

An official in the judging box gave the two contestants word by gesture to go to opposite sides of the posts at the end of the rail. Lennard rode to his end of the field. Marius rode his horse to the other end of the field. When the drums began to sound, the crowds quieted down in anticipation. The drums stopped and a kerchief was dropped to the ground by the starter. Before the kerchief touched the ground, the opponents left their respective areas and charged their horses toward one another. Lennard's lance struck the shield of Marius and was deflected away from him. Marius' lance was thrown off the mark in the same moment that Lennard's lance struck his shield. Both riders remained on their mount.

"Another run!" was the cry from the crowds.

As the two adversaries passed at the midfield, they saluted each other. "Well done, boy!" was the comment that Lennard made to Marius. The young squire took the pass quite capably.

"Thank you, sir," was Marius' reply.

The judges had approved of another run, but a look from Lucio alerted Derkmer, a senior judge, who interrupted the starter. Derkmer shook his head at the starter, indicating that another run would not be granted. This was disappointing to Marius, as he was very competitive and capable of doing better if given another chance. Marius had disappointed Lucio earlier in the day though, and Lucio would not let him forget. The crowd was disappointed too.

It was Brandyn who chose next and he mounted Vento in one fell swoop. He was handed a lance by a young page which he grasped. The young page bade him "Good luck."

When Brandyn looked down from his horse, he said, "Thank you."

The young page smiled back at him. Brandyn smiled back as he turned Vento around and rode him toward the rail. He realized that this young page looked up to him and that he would be setting an example. He rode around the perimeter of the rail until he was on the other side where the knights' tents were. Brandyn was not too familiar with these knights' standards. Some he had never seen before. Brandyn approached the standard that had an ox on it. Brandyn struck this standard. It was the standard of Morden of Aangehert. Morden was the knight who sat in court and you would hardly guess he was there. His hair was jet black, oily and made up a good portion of him. He was slim and unassuming. His eyes, however, could see right through a person. He hardly spoke of his good deeds or at all for that matter. He made an effort to learn what he could. Morden was happier in listening to others stories. He learned a lot from listening to others.

Without ceremony as to draw unnecessary attention to himself, Morden modestly mounted his black steed. The shine off the horse's coat was so bright, it reflected white in places. Morden wore colors of black and silver. The family crest with an ox on it seemed to contrast his slender appearance; how misleading first impressions can be. The knight rode before the grandstand and saluted his majesty before he made his way to his end of the rail. As humble and unassuming as Morden seemed, his arrival at the grandstand happened all too fast. It gave the impression that he was serious and focused. Each contender made his way to the opposite end of the field.

Here was Brandyn at the other end of the rail poised for the joust. He could not see the white of his opponent's eye and yet he knew he was close. Morden did not move a muscle, neither did his horse. The pageantry and crowd, previously occupied in deliberation, food, and drink, were focused on the impending duel. The noise they made sounded like a dull lull over the tournament arena. The drums began to beat, drawing whoever was not tuned to the event to attention. Brandyn was breathing deeper and faster. A sense of fear came over him, but he felt the ring on his finger that was given to him by

Welledon. Having that ring inspired confidence in him.

The honour bestowed upon him by the crowds that gathered and fixed their eyes upon him was inspiring too. There was an inner warmth when he imagined April, as if she was there watching. He removed her kerchief and brought it to his face. The act was so innocent that he did not realise the crowd was paying close attention. Brandyn was awakened by the crowds that took sport with that gesture. "Hey, he's in love!" cried a commoner in the crowd.

Laughter ensued in a burst and carried from section to section like a wave upon the sea. Suddenly the noise ended as if the crowd waited to see his next move so they could poke fun at him. For the moment, Brandyn seemed to lose his focus. Jeremy left his place in the sideline and walked over to him with purpose. He took him by the arm. "There is no time for sentiment now," Jeremy said softly. "Your only focus is him." He turned his head toward Morden. Morden had studied his opponent's gesture. What Brandyn just did had spoken volumes to Morden.

After hearing Jeremy's message, Brandyn took a deep breath and could now hear the crowd again. After returning the kerchief to his breast, he looked over to Jeremy in gratitude. He then grasped the lance specifically made for the sport. Although a real lance that was used in battle was not permitted in tournaments, a tournament lance could hurt a contestant seriously just as well. Brandyn focused on Vento beneath him, the shield in his left hand and the lance in his right. He waited for the indicator that signaled that it was time to ride out.

The drums came to an abrupt stop. The starter dropped the kerchief and off rode Morden as if that was all he had waited for, all his life. Vento was adeptly alert for his master's well-being. Vento had pulled back his neck and stepped back just before the kerchief was dropped. The purpose of this manoeuvre was to alert his rider. It forced Brandyn to tighten his grip on the reins. Vento knew that he would have to start quickly. The steed did not want to lose his rider.

The opponent that they faced would approach them at great speed. Although Vento had gotten him off to an advantageous gallop, Brandyn was having trouble controlling his lance. He managed to lift and keep it lined up and square to his opponent. The wood chopping he did at home earlier that week to stock the woodpile for winter had helped immensely. Morden held back nothing. Morden held his lance down and away as if it would not be any threat. At the last instance he swung the lance up and toward his opponent. He struck Brandyn's shield square on. The shield pushed up right against him. It was Vento's speed that saved the day for Brandyn. The well-aimed lance met with so much resistance due the speed of the rider that it shattered against the shield. The spectators gasped. Brandyn dropped his lance to the ground in order to gain composure on his steed. After a brief, breath taking pause the crowd yelled, "Another run!"

The judges agreed and Lucio was delighted with the idea. He knew Morden. Morden would hold back nothing for a win. If that lance were the kind used in battle, it would not have broken up so easily. A real lance would surely have unseated Brandyn. The two combatants rode back to their starting points. Morden's squire handed him a new lance. Jeremy got a new one for Brandyn from the rack at the field's end. Jeremy handed him the lance and advised, "Steady as she goes. Your lance looked like the wing of a chicken fluttering in the wind. Take hold, get a handle on your lance."

Each competitor had a new lance now. Brandyn noted in that last run that Morden's lance was not directly pointed toward him until the last instance. He too would try this technique. Brandyn had struggled for control of his lance through most of the first run. With the speed of the horse and the length of the lance, it was difficult and heavy to handle. He learned to grasp it securely and use the horse's speed to carry it. Just before impact he would abruptly swing it up, pointed at his competitor. Now that he knew to take early control, he would use what he learned. This time he would carry the lance low and away as if he could not carry the weight of the lance. At the last instant he would swing it up and direct it at his opponent.

Again the drums drew attention to the event while every eye was focused on the field. The drums stopped and the falling kerchief marked the start. Brandyn had learned from Vento to be alert and start away with speed. He carried the lance low and away as he planned. He noted that it was easier to carry that way. He rode and got closer and closer to Morden. In an instant he used the momentum of the ride to swing the lance up toward Morden's shield. At the last instant before the impact, he leaned forward and crouched behind his own shield. Morden had planned on the difficult task of striking Brandyn on his visor. A hit to the visor this time would score the ultimate win. Morden was focused solely on the win that would humiliate and hurt his opponent. On this occasion, however, it was Brandyn's lance that caught Morden's shield. The crowd could see Morden pushed back as Brandyn's lance shattered against the shield of his opponent. In the collision, Morden's lance missed the intended target of his opponent's visor, and for that matter it missed Brandyn entirely. It was Morden this time who had to adjust himself to stay on his horse. It appeared Brandyn was a quick study. To the spectators, the entire action happened so quickly. Oddly enough, it seemed that during the course of the action Brandyn had all the time in the world. It was like time had slowed down. Time was funny that way.

"Another run!" cried the crowd. Lucio wore a blank expression, as he was surprised with the turn of events. "Another run!" the crowd cried. Lucio was against awarding another run because at this point it might go either way. Brandyn was standing out. Lucio chalked up Brandyn's success to beginner's luck. However, Lucio did not want to risk another run that might make Brandyn gain popularity with the crowd. With a look from Lucio, the judges decided to move forward on to the next squire. The crowd was left cheering in anticipation of another run, as this had been a fine display of jousting. Brandyn's trial was over.

Franuch of Solce rode on the field and chose Lennard of Hilroy . Lennard had already combated with Marius to start the event. There was nothing in the rules that said you could not choose a knight that already jousted, so he did. In the battle that ensued, Franuch, due to his rugged build, was able to weather both runs he had with Lennard. In the second run he managed to hit Lennard's thigh by happenstance. Although the afternoon developed into a beautiful warm day, the stress of the challenges, the heat in a suit of armour, the scrunch to his thigh, and his age had taken a toll on Lennard. The pain left him unbalanced as the leg muscles cramped. The proud knight took the pain to his thigh muscles with grace. When the judges ruled a draw, the noble knight returned to his tent.

Benard of Paaxen was the next challenger and chose Pavlen of Dromore, who made knighthood at Blossom Fest earlier that year at Easter festivities. There was a grudge between them over a young woman. Neither of the combatants won over the young woman, but the grudge continued just the same. The young, voluptuous woman, Chelle, was basking somewhere in the crowd. The contest proved to be the most exciting to this point. On the opening run, both their lances shattered against the other's shield. In the second run, both challengers were again approaching with great speed and struck each other simultaneously. On this occasion the lances held firm. Both were unhorsed with a loud thud and crashing of armor that the crowd felt. Both laid on the tournament ground. The incident looked and sounded perilous. Were they seriously hurt, or worse? Had one of them died?

For a moment the crowd was silent as both combatants lay still. Everyone held their breath. Then Pavlen slowly got up and flung off his helmet and dropped it on the ground. He looked toward his adversary. He made his way toward Benard, who lay face up and shaking rapidly on the ground. It looked like a case of broken bones and severed nerve and muscle tissue. Pavlen reached over to lift

Benard's visor to see if he could be of any help. To his surprise he discovered that Benard was shaking due to his laughter. Pavlen offered Benard his hand and helped him to his feet. The grudge was over. The crowd that had held their breath, applauded. They supported each other onto their feet. When each raised an arm toward the crowd, they received thunderous cheers and applause. The fainthearted were relieved to see that apart from bruising that accompanies such activity, no harm had come to either of the pair. The grudge was over. Chelle felt quite anguished that neither man was wounded over her. This particular duel had also cleared, to that point, the tension that accompanies such contests.

For the last contest Keveyn of Strychart, Lucio's pride and joy, rode his horse in ceremony around the rail and tapped the shield of Lennard. There were rumblings amongst the crowd of spectators. Once again Lennard was challenged to joust. Renton, a younger fellow knight, reminded Lennard that he did not have to go, as he had been previously engaged twice and bore some injury to his leg. The judges might have agreed with the decision and ruled that Keveyn should challenge someone else but a glance from Lucio influenced Derkmer. That glance made the challenge acceptable.

Lennard should not have accepted the challenge, but how could he refuse? He could not depend on the judges to protect him. It was obvious whom they served. Renton insisted that he go in his stead but there was the matter of honour. It seems the pressure to perform your duty did not diminish with age. What a person accomplished in the past meant little to the moment. It depended on what a person accomplished lately. Lennard was compelled to perform his duty.

In the very first run Keveyn aimed his lance at Lennard's head to convey that he was going for the win. If a challenger could hit the head of his opponent, it was an automatic win because it was not so easy to do. Instead, Keveyn led Lennard to believe he was going for the quick win but instead dropped his lance at the last instance, catching Lennard's previously injured leg. It was not ethical but most effective at rendering Lennard incapable of continuing.

Unfortunately, Lennard managed to weather the pain that was even greater now. Renton ran over to him and tried to discourage him from continuing. The matter of honour, though, was foremost in Lennard's mind. If he ceased to continue, he would appear old and infirm. He would not walk away from the field of honour with less than what he brought to it.

"There are still a few tricks up my sleeve," the old knight assured Renton.

Renton helped his colleague regain his composure and personally handed him a new lance. Renton was still concerned for this man, who was a worthy role model to him. Lennard rode to his starting post and awaited for the kerchief to be dropped. When the kerchief was dropped, Lennard thought he would surprise his opponent by lifting his misdirected lance at the last moment. The plan was good, but the pain and fatigue prevented him from carrying it out. Lennard could not lift the lance when he needed to. Keveyn, on the other hand, started with the same idea and then lined up his lance to strike Lennard square on his visor. Keveyn's lance found its mark and struck Lennard's visor. The shock of the blow stunned Lennard more than his not being able to lift his lance. In his experience he did whatever it took to stay on his horse because to fall off your horse in battle meant sure death. He instinctively tried to stay on but the blow to the face overruled his desire and ability. Keveyn had scored a win over a notable knight. At his age Lennard should have received better treatment and respect for his contributions to Graedon's realm.

The crowds only see what they see. Although there were those who did not like what they just saw, in the end, everyone likes a winner. There would be talk in the taverns 'til Christmas over this one. To draw the event to a close, King Graedon arose slowly and walked across the platform toward them. The platform overlooked the field where the mounted squires all assembled for the results of the tournament. The judges sent the king a scroll. A page carried a purple pillow with gold fringe carrying the prize for the joust. The trophy was a representation of a knight on a horse fashioned out of copper and plated with silver and gold. Keveyn would also receive the tournament sword for beating out Jeremy of Irminia.

"The winner of the joust, I give you Keveyn of Strychart," announced Graedon. On top of that, Keveyn was handed a tournament wreath, whom he could present to the maiden of his choice from among the crowd of spectators.

To the Victor

The wreath was placed on the end of Keveyn's lance. It seems that Chelle's earlier disappointment was short lived as Keveyn rode over to her section in the stands. Chelle was his choice for "maiden of the tournament game." Keveyn handed her the wreath at the point of his lance. She merely reached out for it and pulled it off the lance. Her attitude and gestures made it look as though this was a routine practice. Chelle placed the wreath on her head to many cheers from the crowd. Everyone beheld the champion of the tournament and his chosen maiden. There were murmurs. There were rumblings in the crowd, however, they were overwhelmed by the thunderous applause connected with the traditional ceremony.

The squires were then called forth for a public ceremony of recognition before the many spectators. The masses would not be on hand during the actual knighting ceremonies at the church the next day. An announcer indicated that Cardinal Spehars would give a blessing and prayer for the candidates. The king, nobility and the gentry all arose from their seats. All that were present in the tournament field and grandstand bowed their heads. The cardinal raised his shepherd's staff and lifted his hands upward. He delivered a prayer over them which most people did not hear. The people waited for an indicator that the prayer was over. At the prayer's conclusion there was an "Amen" uttered which resounded throughout the crowd. The people waited for their king to speak.

There would be a feast at Braemar Castle that very evening. It would not be until the next day, during the rituals of the church ceremony, that the squires would be knighted. At that time the new knights would receive another baptism in water before the church service. The baptism would take place in the Dargell Stream that flowed into Thermanden Bay just behind Braemar Castle. After the baptism they would dress in clean robes and their shining armor before entering the Church of St. Zorren within the walls of Braemar Castle. In church before God, their king and the nobility they would take their oaths as defenders of the faith and servants of the people of the realm. All this would happen on the next day, which was Sunday.

For ceremonial purposes, the brave squires climbed onto the grandstand and assembled themselves before their king. The king arose from his seat. Graedon drew his sword and walked over to the young squires. He raised his arm, thereby lifting his sword over them. In royal fashion King Graedon proclaimed, "In the name of God and St. Michael and St. Zorren, you have earned the right to bear arms and mete justice in the land. It shall be your duty to vanquish ignorance, oppression and selfishness, so help you God."

The new knights each boldly replied, "So help me God!"

So before King Graedon and the people who witnessed, they each swore an oath under God, St. Michael, the archangel and First Knight, and St. Zorren. St. Zorren was a young boy of Peregren who took up arms against a winged serpent that oppressed the people under Lyndorn's reign many years ago. The young boy slew the winged serpent and was proclaimed a knight. By virtue of his incorruptibility, he was later made a saint. When Braemar Castle was built, the church there was named after St. Zorren.

Graedon then walked over to each of them and placed his sword on their shoulder. He tapped each squires' shoulder twice and bestowed upon them their title. He said, "Arise, then Sir Brandyn of Galles. Arise, Sir Franuch of Solce . Arise, Sir Keveyn of Strychart. Arise, Sir Marius of Marmora. Arise, Sir Benard of Paaxten."

Graedon then sheathed his sword in its scabbard and instructed, "Turn and be recognized by the good people of my realm."

When the king raised his arm, the crowds began to cheer again. Brandyn was given the title "of Galles" because he bore the seal of Galles in the ring that Welledon gave him. Welledon made his intentions known to Graedon. Prior to that Brandyn was the only squire in the competition to compete for a knighthood by invitation alone. Not only had Woodcroft, his sponsor, died, but Brandyn did not have a prior deed to land or a title. They say that "the Lord provides." In this case Welledon had resolved that issue on His behalf.

In Honor of a Debt

Now came the issue of paying back the farrier for services rendered. Tom had just the task in mind. He needed logs split for firewood and Brandyn was just the man for the task. It was ironic that bearing the ring of Galles and after being knighted that Brandyn's first task should be to return to a task that involved labor. Brandyn thought about this task for just a moment. He gladly, humbly and gratefully came to his friend's aid. If it was not for Tom's help with Vento, he could not have been as effective in competition. Vento could have been injured. He himself could have been injured. It was an agreement made before he was a knight. Brandyn would keep his word and then prepare himself for the feast at Braemar Castle that evening.

Part of the preparation meant taking a bath with heated water in a large wooden tub in the blacksmith's stable. The tub was normally used to cool the hot fashioned steel. After sweating it out in the tournament events in heavyset armor, Tom suggested that Brandyn take a bath. Melanie, Tom's wife, helped fetch a towel and lye soap made from animal fat and lavender. She also gave Brandyn clean clothing, which was unusual. Tom probably earned a fair wage, but he could not afford to give him clothes. Brandyn had not bathed with heated water before, but he remembered Woodcroft doing so when he was at Galles Castle. It served to sooth sore muscles on the occasion that hot water could be attained for the task. Brandyn would try this hot bathing. Prior to this instance, keeping his hands and face washed when he woke from sleep and before meals had been insisted upon by his mother as a routine. Other than that, swimming in the warmer months was the only bathing he did before.

The new patterned robe of gold and green that he was given was acquired from a weaver in a small shop within the castle walls. It was sent along by Welledon who had chosen it for his new heir. It was a pleasant surprise from a good, wise, old warrior. Welledon knew of Brandyn's debt to Tom but did not settle it. Instead, he asked a favor of Tom. He asked that after Brandyn settled his debt, got cleaned up and asked about the new robe, that he be given a leather purse with an allowance. If Brandyn received the money before settling his debt, he might be tempted to pay Tom without chopping the wood. Welledon was a firm believer in honouring commitments. It showed good attitude and it built character. Despite his position as Duke, he never looked down at doing common chores that needed doing. He had instilled those values in Bram and Woodcroft. To Welledon, chopping wood was easy and relaxing. That might have sounded ridiculous, but remember that a duke has many responsibilities that can weigh down the mind. A return to humble chores was always a good way to experience what his people had to do for a living.

Ballroom Joust

The next item to follow was the great feast in Braemar Castle that evening. Minstrels that bore news of happenings abroad would be there. Magicians that impressed the simple mind with tricks always gained popularity among the castle guests. Apothecaries would sell their soaps and perfumes to promote image. Alchemists would sell their elixirs and tonics to promote good health among other things. The banquet table would be in want of nothing. Everything in the world, to their knowledge, would be on the table and in quite abundance. The dance that followed in the court would be a major event for the ladies of the court. Ladies, young and old, would wear the finest clothing and perfumes that could bewitch the most steadfast uncommitted man. And so the people found food, drink, and entertainment within the king's castle Braemar.

Lucio's mother was present among the noble women of the court. Her name was Vanessa. Vanessa appeared to be younger than her actual years would lead you to believe. She did not speak much but absorbed others' speech like wool in water. She had a keen sense for determining the importance of what was being said. Vanessa was not stunningly beautiful, but her eyes lent mystery to her. Her appearance and manner of speech could arouse men at her will. It was her voice that allured men to her. Vanessa accompanied Lucio from Federic's Court at Peregren when Lucio advanced to the service in Graedon's Court.

As for someone who was beautiful, modest and kind, there was the Princess Elayne. Despite her beauty and kindly demeanour, no knight in the kingdom asked the princess for a dance. They felt that she was above everyone and might be offended by a request for a dance. Everyone seemed to know that asking her to dance would not please Lucio as well, so they stayed away. Even though no knights from the kingdom asked her to dance, that did not stop the visiting dignitary. After having met Jeremy of Irminia in the grandstand at the tournament field earlier that day, Elayne was asked to dance by him. She accepted. Lucio did not approve. Vanessa merely observed. Jeremy escorted Elayne to the dance hall with grace. The two young dignitaries looked rather handsome together. The manner in which they danced drew every eye upon them. They seemed to be dancing on air. The smooth steps and graceful way their bodies followed the music was a pleasure to behold. Lucio did not approve. Jeremy thought how beautiful the princess' face was. Every time the dance called on them to touch hands, how privileged he felt. Elayne had warm thoughts about this brave boy who competed with honour and dignity in the Harvest Moon Fest games. They both wished the dance would never end. Lucio could not wait for it to be over. The truth is, though, neither of them noticed Lucio or anyone else for that matter. Argellor noticed how his nephew was stricken by this young princess. Vanessa merely observed.

Another stricken man was Marius, whose eyes were fixed on the Duke and Duchess of Teresforte's daughter, Bethany. She sat with her mother, the Duchess Martha. Marius could not take his eyes off Bethany. She was a full-bodied young woman. Her face was like that of a baby with green eyes, a thin nose and red lips to rival her flowing red hair. Lucio had hoped to pair her up with Keveyn, but he was nowhere to be found. Keveyn was last seen with Chelle. They should have been present for the opening dance but they were not. It was their duty in honor of tournament victory to start the dance. Since they could not be found, the dance started without them. Marius was careful of his every movement when he danced with Bethany. She was Lord Barton's daughter. Since he was from Marmora, he fell under the lordship of her father. Bethany sensed that Marius was rather reserved despite having the courage to cross the hall and ask for a dance. It was flattering to see Marius so careful and considerate. The girls would get together in groups afterward to discuss and analyze what had occurred that day and evening.

The person most stricken by love's snare was Federics. He had fallen in love with Vanessa in the process of Lucio's guardianship. Since this woman had been oppressed by Sadar, the former Master of Peregren, Federics thought he would be gentle with the woman and her son. For her part she played the role of a lady well in the public eye and at court. The nights, however, belonged to Vanessa. You could not say that she was unfaithful to Federics. They were neither engaged, nor married, nor intended to one another. There was no written or implied understanding between them. However, the more that Vanessa went from lover to lover, the more Federics' love for her grew stronger. Federic's love for Vanessa grew like a weed in a field of grass during a drought. The yearning for her was maddening. He could not understand how Vanessa gave herself to men that did not care about her beyond the present hour. It was consuming him from within although he fought it to keep up appearances. There were many maidens far more young, beautiful, loving and innocent that would gladly have accepted Federics' love. He was a responsible man of twenty-nine years of age with a loyal record of service to Lord Barton and his King Graedon. They had made him the Duke of Peregren. For no practical or explicable reason, he had fallen in love with Vanessa. It was as if a spell had been cast upon him.

As the evening progressed, the ale and spirits promoted a jovial mood as the music played. There were many dances that provided opportunity to mark territory. There were friendly dances among the guests, but here a suitor could show his desires. Vanessa had a modest number of dances with different men from the court. She never seemed too anxious about any suitor. Then Federics stood from his place of honour among the nobility and walked across the open hall in full sight of everyone. He approached the table where Vanessa sat with other beautiful women of the court. Federics asked for the honour of a dance, but she declined politely, turned and continued her conversation with a lady at her table. For Vanessa, who hardly ever spoke at court, it was unusual. Federics, on the other hand, could not speak. After having come a long way across the hall with a heavy heart, he would have to leave alone. It was as if the life had left his body and all that it left behind was a stone in his throat. The look on his face was that of a crushed man. He could not hide his composure. Federics turned and left the scene. In fact, he was absent for the rest of the evening. He did not reappear until the session of the king's court the next evening, where there too he remained speechless.

Baptism by Water and Fire

The next morning there was great anticipation as the nobility and commoners alike gathered to the Church of St. Zorren within the walls of Braemar Castle. Despite the feast the evening before and the cool weather, there were many people gathered there to witness the baptism of Graedon's new knights. The water was quite cold as the new knights made their way barefoot toward the Dargell Stream. The water fell over the rock a good thirteen feet before it flowed into Thermanden Bay. The knights each had a monk from the Bendire Monastery that was assigned to them as they stood at the foot of the waterfall. They each placed their trust in the monks who were clad in modest dark brown attire fastened with rope around their waists. After Cardinal Spehars offered a prayer over them, he asked them the questions of baptism. The knights were to respond to these questions with, "I do."

'Do you believe in God, the Father Almighty, creator of Heaven, the earth and the waters?"

"I do."

"Do you believe in Jesus Christ, our Lord and Saviour?"

"I do."

"Do you believe in the power of the Holy Spirit?"

"I do"

"Do you reject the glamour of evil, all of its snares and refuse to be mastered by them?"

"I do."

"Do you reject sin, so as to live in freedom?"

"I do."

"Do you reject Lucifer, the father of sin and prince of darkeness, and refuse to serve him?"

"I do."

"Do you reject all of Lucifer's works and his empty promises?"

"I do."

"Do you swear to serve the truth without compromise?"

"I do."

"Do you swear to be honorable and promote fairness and justice?"

"I do."

"Do you swear to be generous?"

"I do."

"Do you swear to be chivalrous with all your might and all your power?"

"I do."

"Do you swear to be courtly, to provide safety to men, women, children, and those who cannot fend for themselves?"

"I do."

"It is at this time that I remind you that your oaths are a declaration of your duty and you shall be held accountable for them even at the expense of forfeiting your souls."

The monks took hold of their prospective knight around the shoulders. They pinched the knight's nose and dunked them into the water. The baptism was done.

After the knights withdrew out of the water, they followed the procession of Cardinal Spehars into the gates of Braemar Castle's north wall. The cardinal made his way into the Church of St. Zorren with his procession followed by the nobility and gentry. A crowd of local people followed. On this occasion, as all big occasions, the church would only have standing room at the back. The knights were excused to dress themselves for the special mass to accompany their knighting. When the knights were dressed, they returned in their gleaming armor. They joined the congregation and took their place just before the altar at the front of the church.

There were many prayers and offerings collected to gain favor for the new knights. During the breaking of the bread, a small loaf of wheat bread was blessed by Cardinal Spehars. He gave it to the Assistant Pastor Michaels. The pastor walked over to the knights that were kneeling on the stairs before the altar. He tore off a piece of the bread. He offered it to Brandyn and said, "Corpus Christi."

The phrase meant "The body of Christ." Brandyn replied, "Amen."

Brandyn then took the bread and ate it. Pastor Michaels gave a piece to each of the other knights in the same fashion. Marius, Keveyn, Franuch and Benard each replied "Amen," then took and ate the bread.

After all the knights had received communion, Cardinal Spehars took a gold chalice from the altar and turned toward Pastor Michaels. The pastor filled the goblet with red wine. The cardinal turned and blessed the wine in an antique tongue. After he was finished blessing it, Cardinal Spehars gave the chalice to Pastor Michaels, who walked over to Brandyn and offered it to him. The pastor professed, "Sangue Christi."

The phrase meant "The blood of Christ." Brandyn replied, "Amen."

Brandyn took the chalice in his hands and drank a mouthful of the blessed blood of Christ. Pastor Michaels followed through with each of the other knights. Marius, Keveyn, Franuch and Benard replied their "Amen" and drank of the cup of the blessed blood.

King Graedon got up from his throne behind the altar. He drew his sword and walked toward his new knights. Just like the ceremony after the tournament, he would knight them individually. Graedon started with Brandyn and placed his sword on his shoulder. Graedon moved the sword from one shoulder to the other shoulder and back. The King reminded him, "In the name of God and St. Michael and St. Zorren, I give you the right to bear arms and mete justice in the land. It is your duty to vanquish ignorance, oppression and selfishness." He paused and affirmed, "Arise Sir Brandyn of Galles."

The king repeated himself four more times as he knighted Sir Marius of Marmora, Sir Keveyn of Strychart, Sir Franuch of Solce and Sir Benard of Paaxten.

Matters from Abroad

Later that evening there was a gathering of the dukes and councillors at Braemar Castle in Rothaynen. An emissary traveled to Graedon's court to make him aware of a major crisis. First reported by sailors and now confirmed by an emissary of Leems and an emissary of Craigroyston, that Karnivron, a great warlord from the Nivronian affiliation and his united tribes, were engulfing smaller tribes of people on Tamerana, the great continent. This mighty warlord had started out only as a nuisance, but he was able to unify many nomadic tribes into a single people. This unity gave the tribes more power to bargain with. With his ability to coordinate their military prowess, they became a growing concern. The kingdom of Leems and other established neighbours had to take Karnivron and his people more seriously in their trading and at court. The motivation for Karnivron's actions were strictly for his own ambition to gain power and control over the people.

Karnivron's people were nomadic warriors who not only raided, but traded the commerce they stole. If terms were made which they had agreed to, but they changed their mind about them, they would not honour them. If it meant fighting, they were prepared to do so. An agreement with them might not necessarily be an agreement. They had always fought with their neighbours and amongst themselves. When Karnivron acquired the power to lead the tribe, he realized that if he could keep the people constantly on the move and stop them from fighting amongst themselves, he could consolidate and expand his power. He was clever to devise a law that let the tribes people keep half of all that was pillaged and plundered. The other half was payed in tribute to him. Not only was this a better deal than any prior arrangement that paid out at the discretion of the senior warlords, but it served as an incentive to get more. The more you got, the more you got to keep. The warriors went to war more readily.

In a sense that was how Karnivron consolidated his power. The strong could take what they wanted and keep what they took. When he was young his father was killed in battle. Another warlord took his mother. It was something he had resented but could do nothing about. Nivron, as he was known then, trained harder and longer than anyone else, young or old. He trained with purpose and direction. He thought of his father and what kind of man he may have been. He idealized what a father should be, and naturally his stepfather did not measure up to his expectations. He loved his mother but she now served another man. Nivron was not treated harshly, but if he was going to accomplish greatness, it was obvious that he and he alone would have to earn it. It would not be given to him.

One day, as fate would have it, Nivron and some friends were caught stealing. Nettana, the daughter of the merchant who caught them, compelled them to work off their debt. She had seen these boys in the market and knew that their caper was mere child's play. A jealous warlord sent assassins to kill these boys who were seen with the merchant's daughter, whom he desired. While Nivron and Daminar were away on an errand, one of Nivron's friends was murdered along with the merchant's daughter. Upon learning about the news, he and Daminar, known as "the wise," ran away with a merchant caravan. He knew that his day to avenge would come. He also knew that he would have to be alive to enjoy it. So off they fled, Nivron and Daminar.

After a long absence, Nivron and Daminar returned home. Apart from his mother and younger siblings, he was not missed by his stepfather, Nassifar. He kept a low profile. He weathered his stepfather's indifference by quietly acting as a humble, true and devoted son. As the years passed, his stepfather came to rely on him more and more. Nassifar's own sons, from different wives, lacked stamina, courage or desire. Nivron's physical supremacy to his half-brothers angered his stepfather. Then one day on a large raid, Nassifar had planned on sacrificing Nivron. He would be placed where the men would be in the most danger. He thought, Nivron was sure to die. Instead, Nivron cut Nassifar's throat in the middle of the battle and proceeded to give the orders. In all that confusion Nivron decided it was time that he take over and make the plans. Despite the insurrection within his own army, Nivron pressed on and the battle was won.

Kartiputh, the tribal leader who chose his stepfather to have Nivron's mother, would not be pleased at this breach of command and act of piracy. There was indeed a code of honour that he would have to answer to. Nivron did not take long to provide an answer. Nivron gathered for the aging warlord, the finest women and young virgins from the people they had just conquered. He even convinced his close friends to give up the booty they had looted and stand with him. This, he hoped, would appease and impress the aging, yet still all-powerful tribal leader.

When Nivron presented the spoils to Kartiputh, he and his friends bowed lower than any other warlord. Warlords usually came across as presumptuous and arrogant after a successful triumph. Nivron gained favour with Kartiputh, who saw that his men loved him. Kartiputh saw how Daminar, a wise friend who could easily have his own following, was loyal to him. Over the coming years, Nivron's band of fighting men sacrificed not only their booty but risked their lives as well. They did some of the fiercest fighting when other warlords were content and comfortable in enjoying their spoils as they were growing older and fatter. Nivron's band of men even put down attempts that challenged Kartiputh's leadership when the looting was not so good. The disgruntled war leaders were easy for

Nivron and his close followers to isolate and eliminate. Again, there was no presumption; the spoils were brought to Kartiputh.

For this reason, the complacent Gundernon did not like him. Gundernon did not recognize Nivron as the boy he had wanted to kill over a young girl that he wanted. This was the boy he had forced into exile years earlier. Gundernon was quick to assess who could likely challenge his contention for the leadership of the tribes. He assessed that Nivron was brave, loyal and capable. Ironically, that is the very description of what a leader needs in his ranks, and yet at this moment Gundernon would rather have a less reliable rival.

Kartiputh became concerned about Nivron, his men, his popularity and his ruthlessness. Even the children sang songs of Nivron's adventures. Kartiputh had hoped to have one of his countless heirs make the transition to the throne. None, he feared, could keep the throne for long. So when a suitable heir could not be counted on to keep power over the warlords, Kartiputh had a backup plan. In his wisdom, he arranged for his daughter Caramel to marry Nivron. Caramel was a young girl renowned for her beauty. No suitor could do better.

Gundernon, who was a senior warlord, was upset by this idea. He felt that he was next in line and should have the honour of marrying the young girl. More importantly, he wanted the Karship over the people. A state of civil war in the tribe was festering. The infighting would be welcomed by enemies in the surrounding regions that fell victim to Kartiputh's wrath. Civil war presented an opportunity for them to fight for their freedom. The union, however, would fall apart like a dried cake crumbles in the hand. However, this path would lead to more bloodshed, hardships and be of little benefit for their people as a whole.

Nivron sensed that the time had come to take over; and he did. After the talks, normally the warlords would leave and retreat into their wealth, and make their own plans. Nivron had precalculated the future. He stood his ground and with candour and eloquence, told the people about the future. Nivron spoke of a future that could avoid petty squabbles, spare bloodshed, infighting and resentment amongst themselves. There was complete silence when Nivron spoke. "The enemy is out there, faceless. He seeks to have us do his bidding for him. Can you hear him laughing as we tear at each other over table scraps? Only an experienced man with vision can keep us awake, alert and alive."

Of course this future would depend on good leadership. Gundernon assumed that Nivron was referring to him. He assumed that Nivron who was younger, would take his place and continue to serve him. Gundernon offered, "And you will naturally lead my armies. You have earned the respect of every warlord; women and children even sing your praises."

Gundernon felt that granting him that position and acknowledgement was earned and just. He really did not mean for it to last, for Gundernon did not trust Nivron. The associates of Gundernon, who were familiar with their master, knew that this gesture was a ruse. So did Nivron.

Gundernon, however, had just handed Nivron a reason to oppose him. Nivron wasted no time in turning Gundernon's words against him. "Your armies! How dare you speak such blasphemy before our Kar! Traitor!"

With that mere insult, Gundernon drew his sword just as Nivron wanted. A younger, quicker, prepared Nivron, who also ate less at the feast, quickly positioned himself out of Gundernon's blade swipe. In one quick and ferocious movement, Nivron drew his sword from its scabbard, where it had been waiting patiently. He thrust the blade into Gundernon's stomach with great force. Gundernon was paralysed. Nivron left the blade there and fearlessly turned away and walked unarmed into the path of those who supported Gundernon. They too were paralysed in shock. A few men scrambled for their knives and swords to avenge Gundernon. Before they could take another step against Nivron, they were pierced with arrows. Nivron turned and looked into Gundernon's eyes. He whispered to him softly, "Remember Nettana?"

With that question, Gundernon opened his eyes in greater shock. It all came back to him, he remembered.

"Did she mean anything to you? Did any young maiden mean anything but personal pleasure?" He began to raise his voice. "Now you want Caramel! For all the young girls that you have defiled with your filthy touch, your obese, sweaty body, your rotten breath, breathe no more!"

As if Nivron was demanding that he die in that instant, Gundernon could not take in any breath. It appeared that he died just as Nivron commanded him to do.

Nivron's supporters were poised, prepared, sober and waiting. Those in observance of what had just taken place were awestruck. The fearlessness of this young warlord was spellbinding, yet he still showed respect for the Kar. So before all the remaining assembled tribe leaders and warlords, Kartiputh proclaimed Nivron his son-in-law and added the prefix "Kar" before his name, which implied "royal one." Karnivron took Kartiputh's daughter as his wife and payed homage to the highly esteemed king. Karnivron payed homage to his father-in-law and sought his council on every important matter. It was what Karnivron had sought all his life, someone to call father. All this pleased the assembled tribes leaders and made the transition of power warranted and legal in their eyes.

Karnivron accomplished all this by striking at the head of his enemy. The followers of Gundernon would serve him now in the absence of their leader. Nivron would have had to fight the same tribesman, had Gundernon and his loyal captains survived that night. Karnivron was very happy with Caramel, his lovely betrothed, and he would be good to her while her father lived.

After Kartiputh's death, Karnivron wanted to put an end to any challenge to his karship. He and his closest supporters decided to select a smaller independent tribe and single it out. Then one by one they could annex it or use force to take control. In each instant Karnivron would marry the leader's daughter. His warlords also took women and maidens of high position. This act made the takeover seem less of an invasion and more of a union of sorts. Since the subdued tribe did not want a war, they accepted the new union. There was no one left alive to avenge the fallen. Those who opposed the new leadership or had a negative influence were put to death. If anyone escaped the purging, they were condemned to live outside the tribal family as outlaws.

In the meantime, plans were being made to usurp some other village. All these brides were well looked after. They bore Karnivron many children in the hope that he would choose one child, their own, to be heir to the Kar. The other children of position would serve as councillors and future warriors and uphold the political structure. They all had a vested interest in doing so.

In a short period of years they fought and conquered and united many tribes and clans until the nation would be known as the Nivronian Affiliation. Imagine all those loose tribes and clans affiliated to Karnivron. Affiliated indeed, it would be his offspring who would rule their respective clans and pay homage to their father. Since there were many children, competition was stiff. The family members looked after each other and ensured loyalty to Karnivron. Karnivron was not interested in the oldest male heir but the most capable.

One tribe was lead by his warrior daughter. Mara, who was as beautiful as she was cunning, led a key tribe. The Vallckian tribe that dwelt on the Steppes of Ranamacora, boasted having some of the finest horseman in the entire union. At her father's bidding, Mara took a husband from among the warriors in her tribe. However, her husband perished in battle. She did not take another husband but developed a working rapport with her captains. They all competed for her favour. She rewarded the warrior who was most successful very handsomely but made no commitment. Mara truly was her father's daughter.

Better to Give

In Leems there was great confusion and fear as the Nivronian Affiliation grew stronger. The stronger they grew, the more aggressive they became. The trading terms they proposed became unreasonable and they refused to honour existing ones. The farms in Strachan, on the fringe of Leems, bordering Karnivron's tribes often had their produce raided and stolen. The Nivronian Affiliation had grown in numbers of people. Many of them occupied vacant tracts of land long considered part of Leems. In fact, knights from Leems still policed the region and enforced the king's law. For their part, the foreigners lived in relative peacefulness as they minded the land in their bid to farm, hunt and survive. They kept to themselves.

One of the king's respected knights, Haaron, had to hear a case of a land dispute in one such region. There was an elderly farmer named Desmond and his wife Molly in the southeast of Leems that befriended children of the tribes people who neighbored his land. Like other Leemites, they thought if these neighbors worked and grew their own food, there would be no need to raid their orchards and farms. Over the years Desmond had lent the family of tribes people his experience at farming and in return was aided with their help at labour. Many children died one cruel winter and there was great heartache in the region. Since Desmond and Molly had lost both their children to sickness, he and his wife found consolation with the tribes children. The young children helped with picking apples and pears off the trees. Desmond and Molly grew fond of them. The young children especially liked when the apples were pressed to make cider. The look of joy on the children's faces was reward enough for them. The children enjoyed drinking the fresh pressed apple cider.

There was never an agreement even discussed as to the stewardship of Desmond's land. Desmond and Molly were looking for a buyer to sell their land to. They preferred to go live with Molly's younger brother's family in the Kilkenny Castle region to the north. The tribes people anticipated that the land would pass on to them by virtue of their having helped Desmond. Desmond and Molly had no relatives interested in moving to the southeast part of Leems. Other Leemites were not interested in relocating so close to the nomadic tribes that lived in the area either. So the tribesman that neighbored Desmond's land just encroached and presumed to occupy the farmland and take what they wanted from the orchards. Desmond sent word to White Brick Court in Kilkenny Council. "I would like to think that it is my idea to invite people to or give away produce from my land."

When Haaron, the knight from the king's court, held a session to hear the arguments in the dispute, he made an allowance for the rights of the squatters. Desmond lost a portion of his land in the ruling. In reality, the decision was based on land usage. Although the land had been owned by Desmond, the tribes people had worked and come to depend on the land for years. As prescribed, Leems' law stated that if a person worked land for a period of greater than five years and there was no dispute made by the owner of the said land, then the person had rights to such land usage. In that time the tribes people became dependent on produce from the land to survive. The judgment was meant to appease the tribes people and illustrate that their treatment on Leems' lands was just and fair. It was also made with Desmond and Molly in mind because despite the fertile soil, there were no interested buyers who wanted to move to that region. The aging landowner would be responsible for taxes, which he might not be able to pay without help from these very neighbours to gather his produce and sell it. The judgement called for cooperation and mutual understanding. As insightful as the judgement was, the decision neither got the appreciation it merited from the tribes' people nor did it please Desmond and Molly.

News of the decision, however, made its way to Karnivron. He who heard about everything involving his nomadic people was most impressed with the wisdom of this Haaron. Haaron's judgment was just and true. The judgment was a foundation for peace and cohabitation. Daminar, "the wise," spoke favorably of the decision. He praised its author and had respect for him. Karnivron trusted his advisor's advice implicitly. It certainly was an honour to be recognized and respected by an enemy. In this way the reputation of Haaron grew.

Haaron and his devoted knights and soldiers also defended against attacks on Leemite villages by warlords in Karnivron's Union. The attacks were not sanctioned by Karnivron. Karnivron felt that as long as his tribes did not attack each other, fighting was of no consequence to him. Haaron's knights repeatedly managed to repel the enemy and keep order in this troubled part of the kingdom. To fail even once would mean ruin for Leems. How long could this last, and what if these warlords united?

As his reputation grew favourable with Karnivron and Daminar, all their warlords and captains hated this Leemite knight. Each wanted to be the one to defeat Haaron and thus make a name for himself before their great Karnivron. Perhaps they could impress Mara and would then be the next "Kar." If only they could crush this Haaron. His daughter Mara grew more interested in this wise warrior whose reputation preceded him. She took a keen interest and wanted to learn more about him. She wanted to meet him.

After the court decision, Desmond and Molly never went to live with their kin. The need to stand up to their neighbours and for their rights made them bitter. The tribe's children, who grew up amidst this elderly couple, treated them with indifference, ignored them and even played pranks on them. Desmond and Molly also had taken for granted the help they used to get from the tribal settlers who became their neighbours. The help they used to get from the tribal settlers was withheld. There was more and more work for them to do, so their bitterness grew.

More and more people from the tribe came to the region in search of food. More and more trees were cut down to make way for farmland and to be used for fuel in cooking and keeping warm. What they did not realize is that with the clearing of the trees of the ancient forest, new disease spread as the homes of animals were disturbed. The animals they disturbed and displaced were not only large but very, very small.

With more numbers of people moving into the area, every adolescent in the tribe wanted to make an impression for their peers. A common dare was to disturb the Leemites. One night while their homestead and orchards were being raided, Desmond got so upset. He tensed up, ran out and began to shout. In that excitement he put his hand to his chest, turned to look at Molly and then fell to the ground and died. After his internment, which was attended by the Leems' farming community, Molly packed what she could carry and left for her brother's homestead near Kilkenny Castle. The departure would foreshadow things to come.

A Court Divided

The news of the sweeping growth in power of Karnivron caused a great divide among King Graedon's advisors, the knights, the court and the people of Rothaynen. Arno, the emissary, on behalf of King Henrickard of Leems, wanted to secure support against Karnivron. The fertile lands of southwest Leems would be lost to the nomadic tribes if he could not secure support. In Graedon's Court there was disunity, disloyalty and distrust. Even King Graedon was indecisive. He had not recovered from his illness. He wavered in his course of action. There was a plea for a navy of their own to be built. The recent attack on Wendover was a perfect reason to build a navy. Brandyn had hoped that a castle fortress to guard Mead and the Wendover Lowlands be commissioned. These projects were all worthy suggestions, but they take planning, time and finances. With this threat to King Henrickard of Leems, they could not undertake them all. Graedon was torn between the advice of his successful, daring captain and his lifetime friends and advisors, who were growing fewer in number. His ambitious captain of the guard, Lucio, argued that they lacked the ships to send an army to Leems in Tamerana, the great continent. The best course of action was to engage emissaries to open talks with the mighty warlord Karnivron.

Tonio the emissary from Craigroyston, replied, "If it is ships that you require, My Lord King Jonquis has authorized me to extend passage on our naval vessels."

Lucio retorted with a humanitarian tone, “Karnivron’s people are hungry and they need food. That is why they attack.”

Lord Welledon replied, “They are hungry alright, but for conquest. These people never think twice about killing at will for a simple bauble, and it is encouraged by their leader. How do you think he gained power?”

Federics broke his silence and spoke in support, “There is no doubt that if the Leemites are conquered, it may not be long before they attack us. We have no ships to meet them on the open seas. We do not know their numbers or when they will attack. If they attack us someday and we lose, they will enslave our people into servitude.”

“We have had raiders from Tamerana before. Their raids on Petrinvincit were senseless. The real prize lay in the fields of Marmora where garden produce abounded, but they kept butting their heads against the mighty fortress walls. If they had breached our defences, no doubt they would conquer, kill and destroy whatever they could not carry with them,” affirmed Lord Barton.

“Perhaps because they were desperate for food to survive. Danger seems to matter little when innocent women and children are starving,” Lucio summed with an empathetic tone. “Besides, they have no naval vessels of their own,” he added.

The entire hall was pensive and it looked as though Lucio’s plan for diplomacy would carry the day; it was certainly favoured.

The people of Graedon’s realm had just worked for their portion of comfort and were preparing for winter. The royal granaries were filled with a healthy harvest yield. The thought of preparing for war, let alone traveling across the sea in late fall, was the last thing on anyone’s mind. They had recently routed the Huynstens and the Orgols.

Lord Barton pressed, “It is perhaps that you cannot remember the ruthlessness and insatiable desire of these warlords to conquer more and more and subject people to do their will. They have no regard for the women and men that they sell into servitude. They kill all children who may someday oppose them. Those who cannot defend themselves or become old or infirm and not able to work are left to toil until they die or are put to death. The Kingdom of Leems is now threatened!"

"Then let them fight for their land. If we go, what do we get out of it?" challenged Varden, a good knight who was obviously tired. The drink that he thought might relax him had made him easy to irritate.

Lord Barton answered, "What did King Jonquis acquire from having his navy do battle with the Huynsten ships late this summer? Remember, we are honoured by the presence of Jonquis' envoy." He paused and acknowledged Tonio, then continued, "We had a common enemy. Trade ships from Craigroyston were being disturbed and the people of the Wendover Lowlands region faced an invasion. Jonquis' did not ask 'what will "I" get out of it'?

"Selwyck could have gotten away with his three ships unscathed. It was not their fight that day. They were not in any danger. They elected to help. They elected to do a good thing. Does anyone think we could have easily routed the Huynstens that day without Selwyck's help that challenged the Huynsten ships? How many of us would be absent today if it were not for decent consideration? Would we still be fighting and waiting within our castle walls for them to attack? Would we have retreated and given up Wendover because the force that arrived was overwhelming? No, cousin," he turned to King Graedon, "it is our duty and obligation to help King Henrickard morally. It is a decent and considerate thing to do. We are familiar with his people. They have traded fairly with ours. More so, Henrickard's son Mattic is married to Jonquis' sister, Ellen. Jonquis has already shown good faith in helping us. No, My Liege, if Jonquis and Henrickard should have an enemy, then I say that enemy is our enemy. He needs our help and time is crucial when preparing and sending an army. Our hesitating is a backhanded slap against this just and true monarch to our north and the God-fearing people of Leems, and eventually, to ourselves."

These words from the silver-haired man awakened every person in the king's hall. These words shamed the infirm of purpose, but Lucio insisted that a peaceful means must at least be attempted. Those who were tired, weary of battle and had no real grasp of politics without difficulty sided with Lucio. Lucio went further to suggest that, "If His Majesty wills, I will lead the delegation to speak with Karnivron. We will bring vessels of foodstuffs to feed the children of his realm." Lucio volunteered because he was confident that Graedon would not send him anyway.

Lord Barton was infuriated as many brave fighting men were killed defending the sovereignty of the realm. He charged, "Welledon has lost both his sons in defence of our sovereignty. Karnivron is no different than the pirates from Orgol, Huynsten, Skarsgaard or Hammersgaard. How many others laid down their lives for the safety of our realm?"

Barton questioned firmly, "They fail to secure food from our granaries when they try to take it by force, and now we are going to give it to a people who do the same to Leems. We are going to give it to them, not trade but give it to them? How do we explain this to the valiant fighting men who fell in an attempt to protect our people and our interests? That suggestion is ludicrous. It borders on stupidity!"

"War mongers," retorted Lucio in anger. "War mongers!"

The wise old Lord Barton would not stand for it, and he continued to lash out against Lucio. "It is treason! Treason I tell you!"

Lucio had not faced resistance since his days with Sadar. He got used to getting his own way. Being offended before the members of the king's council, Lucio drew his sword in anger. He literally could not control his emotions. He had lost his composure. In his rage and in the commotion that ensued, he would surely have slain Barton. Lucio raised his sword in anger to thrust it at Barton. It was Brandyn, who, thinking quickly, flung a plate that caught Lucio's wrist, forcing him to drop his sword in flight. Lucio grabbed his wrist with his other hand and tried to comfort his arm.

Although Brandyn saved Lord Barton, injury and insult had befallen the daring captain who served his king capably. Had Lucio not served Graedon and his realm loyally?

Had he not cleverly delivered victory after victory keeping the kingdom's enemies at bay?

Had Lucio not trained the squires and overseen armament production?

Had Lucio not coordinated the transfer and distribution of grain that the kingdom would rely on to endure the winter?

The knights were divided between those who would have immediately run Brandyn through with their swords, and those who scrambled to maintain order. Keveyn and Franuch immediately rose against Brandyn. It was Renton and Lennard that just happened to be sitting close by who intervened between Brandyn and harm. In court the nobles seized the opportunity to open old wounds, churn and leash out with issues that should have long been forgotten. Fear governed where the people were concerned and the stronger you were, the more you could press your advantage.

With the division and indecision that transpired, it would seem that their enemy had already won. Tonio, the emissary of Craigroyston, was not impressed with the lack of diplomacy. Tonio had witnessed somewhat the same disorder in Craigroyston with the return of Selwyck from that very naval battle they referred to. Tonio was grateful, however, for the straight, honest manner in which the council members spoke. It certainly let him know where they stood. He could now return and report to King Jonquis and Queen Enyja. In his mind, Tonio was certain that Selwyck had done the right thing when he burned the *Bravada* in a funeral rite. The behavior that he witnessed was not that of a grateful people. Tonio still believed that Selwyck's attack on the Huynsten ships was the right thing for the greater good, however, it did not seem to him that Graedon's council understood the greater good. The greater good would take sacrifice, unity and selflessness. Most of Graedon's council was not willing to sacrifice anything. Arno, the Leemite emissary, gathered as much.

After order was restored to the king's court, there was a demand that Brandyn be held accountable for his offensive act against Lucio. To shift the emphasis off the real problem, they turned to account for the behaviour of a newly made knight. He was made to apologize and willingly did so. However, he explained how it seemed that Lucio might have struck Lord Barton. Lucio claimed that he drew his sword in an attempt to restore order to the assembly. Lucio stated calmly the he would never have used his sword on any noble, let alone the king's cousin. That is not how Barton saw it. Matters were not right for the assembled courtiers. Brandyn had done the right thing. He had been concerned for Lord Barton's safety. Brandyn did not harm Lucio in a lasting manner. In reality, Lucio lost his composure. He had meant to swing his sword at Lord Barton. Were the lords so tired with drink and full stomachs that they could ignore the implication of this display?

Lucio, the king's advisor, had just threatened a prominent duke, the king's cousin no less. Had they forgotten about what nearly happened to Lord Barton?

What about the attack on Lord Barton?

Lucio quickly apologized to the king for having lost his temper, and drawing his sword in the first place. He reasoned that, "Lord Barton is an older statesman and I should have shown more respect. I drew my sword as a symbol for restoring order. I do regret it now." He paused and then continued, "As for Brandyn, he did intervene where he thought he should. This young knight has served as a squire to our beloved Woodcroft and recently distinguished himself in the games. There is no doubt about his allegiance to the King and his court and we too are friends." Lucio appeared pensive and reflecting on what had just happened. The court was silent as they watched him bow his head humbly. Barton and Welledon could see right through Lucio's coyness.

The ailing king, however, was quick to accept Lucio's apology. Lucio exhibited brilliant diplomacy. Although, Barton, who was portrayed as old and infirm, remained offended. Barton did not press the matter, however, because order had just been restored and he did not trust all the knights gathered there. They were all irritable and snapped at any idea that was not supported by Lucio. Even at the Wendover campaign and the one in Mead, there seemed to be a power struggle over who was in charge of the army. In his mind Barton questioned whether it was the drink or their will or both.

In vino veritas; perhaps they were showing their unconditional support for Lucio. The King, though, was anxious for a peaceful solution, and Lucio seemed the courtly man of the hour though chiefly responsible for the ruckus. In truth, Lucio had not forgiven Lord Barton nor Brandyn, and he would kill them both when the opportunity arose.

Graedon had reached a conclusion. "With the winter upon us the conditions to send an army to cross the sea to Leems would be perilous. It would take weeks to prepare weapons and food. That would take us into late November. The good emissaries also realize that it is perilous to travel by sea in November. The army we send may be engulfed by the sea. Even our enemies refrain from attacking us during the winter months. We would also be reliant on ships from Craigroyston to transport our fighting men. In the meantime and if possible, I support avoiding an all-out war. If the people of Leems will hold out through these winter months, their resolve will be joined by the forces of Rothaynen. If not, we will have to embark to Leems with Jonquis just before winter's end."

"If I may speak, Your Majesty," came an appeal from Arno, the emissary of Leems.

"Please do, honoured ambassador," replied Graedon.

"Our enemy does not have to wait for favourable conditions of the sea to attack us. We are, as you know, landlocked with them. A single divide in the mountain is what stands between the Strachan ramparts in southeast Leems and the juggernaut. After the ramparts of Strachan, the terrain is farmland as far as Kilkenny Castle. On the other side of that mountain is a force so large that it cannot be counted. They have no castles and their homes are completely mobile. They can attack with fury and great numbers from any direction. I can assure His Majesty that we are not a provoking or unreasonable people. Diplomacy has already been employed by our great knight, Haaron, and yielded little result. It seems after skirmishes, Haaron can only maintain order. We are losing ground, literally. Karnivron's warlords feel they are invincible. If attacked, all Haaron could do is supervise a retreat. All they need is a reason for a full war, and a reason can be made. The number in his armies grow and so does their strength. They have but to merely want something to take it. If help is to come from your kingdom, we must have it sooner than later."

The entire king's council had been quiet while Arno relayed the circumstances. Graedon took into account that in the time since Lucio left Peregren, productivity in weapons manufacture had declined. The decline was due to indifference and labour disputes. Defending against the Huynsten attack at Wendover and Mead exhausted the supply of weapons. More so, productivity at Peregren was not optimum. Graedon knew that he would need more time to rearm. He did not want that information to be known by anyone, especially the visiting emissaries. Graedon replied to Arno, "My good emissary, it is not a matter of will, but after having fought to defend our own kingdom, we will need time to rearm ourselves. For the moment, I am prepared to send a small delegation to accompany you to Leems. At the bidding of our delegation we shall try to meet with and discuss differences with Karnivron. His numbers may be greater than yours at present, but he will have to consider the skilled armies of Galles, Teresforte, Peregren, Braemar and Craigroyston's too."

Graedon had just inferred commitment of his armies to the aid of Leems. The plan was not without merits and seemed reasonable. Although the statement was verbal, it was the best that Arno would accomplish that day. "If Your Majesty will then excuse our delegation, we shall prepare for our journey back. With affection for the king and his people, we take your leave," Arno replied to Graedon.

"If Your Majesty will excuse me, I too must prepare to return to Craigroyston," Emissary Tonio added.

"Before you leave, Lucio will assemble a delegation to send to Leems. If you could, give them passage on your ships. We will draft a letter to inform both Jonquis and Henrickard of our plans, and you may bear it to your respective kings. It will be ready for both of you before you leave in the morning. A safe journey to you; may you be in God's care," said Graedon.

"Your Highness," they both declared, bowed in respect and took their leave.

Needs and Wants

After Arno and Tonio left, the discussion turned to the issues of building a navy and a fortress at Wendover to the east or Mead to the south. As for the building of a navy, Graedon had a proposal for King Jonquis. He thought that if they could purchase a naval vessel, for the time being it could be studied for design. In the meantime, wood from Galles or north of Teresforte could be gathered to Marmora for the task of building their own navy. Lord Barton remarked, "The strongest wood comes from the woodlands to the north of Teresforte or in west Galles."

Argellor came from a maritime island and, having experience in both building and sailing sea faring vessels, expressed, "The mighty oaks of your region are truly strong, but their nature is also dense and heavy. When oak wood is immersed in water for long periods it takes on water and makes it even heavier. On top of that, over time oak wood cracks and rots. Although this material would be ideal for the ribs of the vessel, there is cedar wood on the isle of Irminia that would be more effective for the body of the boat. The very same wood that abounds in Roysford." Roysford was the western part of Craigroyston where indeed a boundless forest of cedar trees had hardly been disturbed.

"As we have just heard," Graedon realized, "there is a lot more to building a ship than just building a ship. Not only is the design important, but the specific materials to use and construction skills as well. We are going to need the help of our friends." He, of course, referred to Jonquis in Craigroyston and Tosham, Duke of Irminia, who was Argellor's brother. Graedon thought to himself, *if only they could have kept Selwyck's ship, the* Bravada, *instead of using it for the funeral rites.* The *Bravada* could have been used as a model template. Selwyck had been firm with his resolve though. The custom of cremation was used in Craigton; he was from Roysford where the dead were buried in caves or interred in the ground. Selwyck had chosen the route of cremation to avoid the naval vessel falling into another kingdom's control. He had done the wise thing.

The discussion was taking its toll on the ailing monarch. Graedon stood up, as he was tired and lightheaded. There was also the insistence about the building of a castle at Mead or Wendover. It would be ideal to build both, but in reality they could only begin work on one for now. The next sensible progression was to build a castle and granary storehouses at Mead to the west of Wendover. Mead grew barley grains and specialized in the brewing of ales and single malt spirits. Mead was closer to Braemar Castle and could be supported easier for that reason. It made good sense. Wendover would have to wait.

If a castle and granary were built at Wendover, which was farther away in the far southeast, it would take more travel time to support. A castle at Wendover could be put under siege by a large naval supported invasion. The Huynstens nearly accomplished that. Worst of all, if Wendover fell, then a castle there would be used as a fortress to shield the enemy. With plenty of food supplies already present in the region, a captured castle at Wendover could easily be the point of launching an assault against Braemar Castle at the heart of Rothaynen. To build a castle at Wendover would require a navy to be in place already. The next logical location for a castle would be Mead by virtue of its vicinity to both Braemar, the Gallesian Forest and Wendover. If an invading force landed at the Mead coast, a castle at Mead could be supported easier. It was a disappointment for Brandyn to hear, but he understood the reasoning.

Although it was before sunset, it was late, and Barton would normally have stayed the remainder of the evening and spent the night. Given the ruckus at court, Barton was not too happy with the matter. Barton felt it would be better to set out for Teresforte. Even though it meant setting up camp before midnight, Barton decided to leave the castle's comforts. Argellor and Jeremy left with Lord Barton to return to their ship that was anchored at Marmora. The ship had traded its cod stock for cabbage and orchard fruits. It was disappointing for Jeremy, who wanted to see the Princess Elayne the next morning. Barton, in his gratitude for being saved, suggested that Brandyn to come to Teresforte, for he sensed that Lucio might take vengeance on him. Barton perceived that the loyalty of the army toward Lucio was very strong. Brandyn's invitation to Galles stood by virtue of the ring he wore. Welledon, however, understood this boy's zeal to return to Wendover for the girl who gave him the kerchief. In his youthful pride Brandyn gracefully declined Barton and Welledon, for he reasoned that the discord was over, the peace had been made, and a knight's word was his bond. How naive Brandyn was. When Barton and Welledon departed with their forces for their castles and evening fell, Brandyn would learn just what the word of Lucio was worth.

A Knight in the Castle

He would have liked to go with Welledon to Galles, but Brandyn could not wait to set out for Wendover. He could not wait to see April. He had such good news to bring to her. Their dream was starting to come true. Malcolm and Andrea would be proud parents. Meaghan could take comfort that this knighting would not have been possible without her "Wills." In the end, they all should have stayed at Braemar Castle and supported Graedon, their king. It was late October, the grains and produce were collected and safe. It was a good harvest and winter's blanket would make life slow down. Who could foresee what was to come?

Before departing, Barton had a word with Graedon about keeping an eye on Brandyn. He did not want any retaliation against him. Barton did not want to stress the king over the incident at court, but he told Graedon, "You may have to go fishing." Graedon never went fishing. He did not enjoy fishing. The phrase was strange advice to give an ailing person, but there was a deeper meaning which the two kindred persons understood. Welledon had the same idea and reminded Graedon that he had given Brandyn the ring with the seal of Galles. With that, Brandyn was given a room in the castle in the wing where dignitaries and special guests retired to sleep. In that wing, there were guards posted in the corridors to assure safety. Graedon reassured both Welledon and Barton that Brandyn was as safe as he was.

The halls had a watch around the clock. From the balcony on the way to Brandyn's room you could overlook the king's court and ballroom. The sight was endearing with the carpets and tapestries and curtains that hung and added colour to the great hall. The wood mouldings added warmth to the stone walls and Brandyn thought, *if only one day they could build a castle in Wendover, I would be happy*. He was escorted down the hallway and a large key unlocked the heavy door to the room that he was to inhabit. The court page assigned him a key of his own that could lock the door from the inside for privacy. Another servant brought an extra bed blanket, a vessel of water, a basin and a towel. After all that had transpired, he was so tired that he had to force his eyes open to wash his hands, splash water on his face and dry up before he could collapse on the bed.

As comfortable as the bed was, he could not sleep. It was so easy a moment earlier, but now he could not sleep. Despite his being tired when he lay his head on the feather pillow, his eyes opened wide. It actually hurt to close them and he was more comfortable to keep them wide open. It was his conscience trying to tell him something, but he ignored it. He assumed that he was safe. As the time passed though, he got more comfortable and began to rest. There was only one person he could think of. There was only one place he would rather be. He thought about the fields of golden wheat and April's long, flowing hair as she walked through it. He saw her hands, face, eyes and the shape of her mouth. He remembered pressing his lips to hers and holding her to himself. He remembered how it felt. He could not imagine holding anyone else. He did not want anything else. The court, the kingdom and the whole world was facing a threat to peace and freedom and all he could do was think of April.

He might have nodded off, but he heard the lock turn gently and the latch on his chamber door lift slightly. Someone was going to a great deal of trouble not to make noise, but the old heavy latch cried out in lament to what was about to happen. The assassins entered the room, for there were two of them. What light there was, came from the torch in the hall outside. Brandyn could see their faces as one smirked. He could see the daggers they hoped would help them do the dirty deed they wanted done.

As they approached, closer and closer and closer still, Brandyn tossed the heavy quilt over one assassin and reached for the handle of the wooden water bucket. As the other assassin leaped forward with his dagger, Brandyn swung the bucket and caught him in the face. The assassin dropped the dagger and put his hands across his face to support the pain. Meanwhile, the other assassin got free of the quilt, but Brandyn threw upon him what water remained in the bucket. As the man fumbled in the dark, Brandyn swung the bucket by the handle and conked him on the head with it.

With all that calamity, the guards on that level came and entered the chamber. They brought with them a torch to better illuminate the room, and each had a spear with an axe head at the top. Brandyn reached for his clothes and began dressing himself, since he could not do so earlier. Brandyn began to explain what had happened. As he turned his back to the guards and was fixing his vestments, he walked toward the mirror and looked into it. Just in time he threw himself out of the path of the spear which the guard threw at him. The spear broke the wood moulding and shattered the mirror. He realized that treachery was evident. He had to get out of there. The guard who threw the spear charged toward him. Brandyn quickly moved out of the way, and using the guard's momentum, he pushed the big man's head into the stone wall. The other guard was attacking with his spear. Brandyn quickly grabbed for the spear with his hands. The two adversaries tried to wrestle the spear away. After stopping his opponent's advance, Brandyn outmanoeuvred him by releasing his right hand from the spear. With it he struck low at the aggressor's stomach. After the guard bent over to grab his stomach, Brandyn regained his hold on the spear. With it he bashed the attacker's helmet with the side of the axe head and knocked him out cold. All he could think was, *I have got to get out of here*. He went into the hall and saw the stairway leading down and up. If he went down that would lead him through the great hall; surely someone would see him and probably attack him. Who could he trust?

If he went up, *Well, who knows?* he thought. He just ran and took the stairs two by two. He took the stairs so swift and light on his feet that you could not hear him.

Meanwhile, other castle guards checked on what had happened in Brandyn's room. You could not tell which guards were loyal to Lucio or served the king. They brought a torch with them. One ran to the window to see if Brandyn had escaped by that means. The guards searched the room and looked behind the tapestries to see if Brandyn was hiding. Then they rushed into the hall and proceeded down the stairs. In their pursuit they were almost stopped cold by the outline of an eerie image that was coming up the same staircase that they so hurriedly wanted to descend. It was Lucio.

"He has eluded you," he said calmly in a deep voice as he invoked fear in them.

"Well, we know he has not come this way," Lucio continued with sarcasm since he had just come from there.

At that the guards immediately turned and rushed upstairs.

All the while, Brandyn had scaled the stairway to the top and ran down the hall into a corridor. There were tapestries on the walls and the sight of two guards stopped him in his tracks. It took his breath when he saw them. Fortunately, they were asleep. Unfortunately, behind him the guards were in pursuit. Brandyn looked up and saw the supporting beams overhead. He climbed around and over the sleeping guards to use the stone around the doorway to climb up to the beams. The noise he made did not disturb the sleeping guards, however, the occupant behind that chamber door arose, gathered a robe and went to the door to listen closer. As Brandyn pulled himself onto the wooden brace, some dust fell down. Some of the dust landed on the guard's face. The guard was disturbed to the point of sneezing, which awoke his cohort, and just in time too. The search party of guards arrived.

"Has anyone been here?" belted out a voice with authority.

Naturally, the guards answered honestly that no one had been by there. Lucio, who followed up the stairs, studied them for a moment. Lucio noticed some thick dust on the guards uniform and the smell of ale on their breath and gave a look of disgust. He then reassigned them to cover the route down the stairs while he proceeded forward down the hall. Lucio thought, *How could Brandyn have disappeared?*

Brandyn's present location was safe for now, but eventually in daylight he would be discovered. Brandyn thought if he went back to his room he could find a way out the window somehow. It was a plan and no other was available since he could not go down the stairs or across the corridor. With easy agility he climbed down from the beams. Brandyn was startled by the tenant of the chamber who had opened the door slightly. He froze.

"Get in quickly," whispered a soft voice with authority as she opened the door more. It was a girl, but not any girl. It was the Princess Elayne.

"Quicky, get in," she reaffirmed. She immediately recognized him from the games. He was the squire who had competed with Jeremy at swords.

Brandyn entered in a hurry. She closed the heavy door, bolted and locked it. Her door did not make a noise at all. In all that excitement the princess' attendant was still fast asleep. She was on her bed off to the side of the princess' bed. Ornelda was snoring.

By this time the search party returned and were knocking on the princess' door. The knocking would surely awake the attendant so the princess Elayne quickly showed Brandyn to the tapestries and he hid him behind them. She then entered her bed as if she had been asleep all the while. At that point the knocking awoke the attendant, who promptly went to answer the door. "Just a moment," she uttered as she made her way to the door. "I beg your pardon but the princess is sleeping!" Ornelda exclaimed in a whisper.

"Ornelda," the princess softly asked. "Who is there?"

"You have awoken her!" she lamented as she opened the door wider.

"I beg your pardon, madam, but it seems there is an unworthy guest among the household and as it is my duty to protect the members of this household..."

"Why, is that you Captain Lucio?" the princess interrupted. "What brings you here at this hour?" she said from her bed as though awakening from a deep slumber.

"Call me Lucio," he told her, but being referred to as Captain Lucio from the princess was impressive he thought. "Forgive me, Your Highness," he continued, "but we are in pursuit of a thief among us."

"A thief?" questioned Elayne.

"Yes, we chased him across the great hall, where he made his way up this stairway and perhaps across your corridor," Lucio lied convincingly.

"And did you find him?" asked Ornelda.

"No, he seems to have alluded us for the time being. We thought perhaps he might have gotten into your room."

"Really, Captain, you cannot be serious," said Ornelda, who was rather offended.

"I was asleep," replied the princess.

"But I was not," Ornelda interrupted abruptly. "If you are quite done, it is not ladylike to entertain a party of men at this late hour." She continued under her breath, "Nonsense, utter nonsense."

Lucio spoke to the princess. "Naturally, I do apologize for barging in like this at this late ho—"

"Then good night, Captain," interrupted Ornelda firmly.

Lucio turned and indicated for the guards to withdraw. The guards withdrew from the chamber and Lucio had just enough time get out. He turned to bid the princess goodnight, but before he could do so, Ornelda shut the door firmly in front of him. Some loose dust fell down from the beams. Lucio looked up and surmised how Brandyn had escaped.

Plan of Escape

When all had settled down and the corridor was clear except for the guards stationed outside to protect the princess, Elayne revealed her secret to Ornelda. “Be quiet,” she spoke softly and placed her finger to her mouth. She then walked toward the colorful tapestry on the wall and pulled it back to reveal Brandyn. He was grateful for what the princess had done. Ornelda’s eyes opened wide in shock to discover this fine young figure of a man hiding in the princess’ chambers. In fact, she could not speak.

“Is it because I made you lie to Lucio ?” queried the princess.

“Of course not,” she retorted, “I could not care less about that snake. What would your father say? How did he get in here? How long has he been here?”

“Perhaps I should answer these questions.” Brandyn said, “I am Brandyn of the Wendover Lowlands and as of recently a new knight and heir to the Dukedom of Galles.”

“Another suitor for Elayne’s hand, no doubt,” interrupted Ornelda. “A new knight, wet behind the ears yet dashing and handso—”

“Just let him explain, Ornelda. He was in trouble,” conveyed Elayne.

“What about that Irminian lad?” she questioned. “I thought he was a courtly figure. He cast a fine shadow.” Of course she was referring to Jeremy whom the princess danced with in the great hall. His uncle Argellor had introduced Jeremy to Graedon and Elayne.

"Please, madam, allow me to explain," started Brandyn. "My name is Brandyn. I was lucky enough to be invited in here at the last minute. You see, someone is trying to kill me. I could have been on my way to Teresforte or Galles but decided to stay the night before I set out for Wendover. During court I—"

He was interrupted, "You are the one who flung an apple at Lucio, aren't you?"

It was strange how a story could get changed.

"It was a plate," he replied.

"No matter, I don't like that Lucio. From the day he came here, he has not impressed me in the least. Nor that witch he calls his mother."

"Ornelda!" scolded Elayne.

Ornelda affirmed, "I don't like him or his mother. She has been responsible for many quarrels over her." She paused sarcastically. "Honour."

"Ornelda!" scolded Elayne.

Ornelda turned to Brandyn and asked, "So who is trying to kill you?"

"Lucio. You see, when I was asleep, that is I should have been asleep but could not, you see, there is a girl I have to get home to."

"Our princess is not good enough for you," challenged Ornelda, because she immediately liked Brandyn.

"Oh, no, madam, the princess is very beautiful. You see, the door to my chamber opened and I saw two assassins enter."

"Did you recognize them? Had you ever see them before?" inquired Elayne.

"My dear, you are going to have to stop interrupting the boy if we are to find out anything," scolded Ornelda.

"I got a glimpse of the face but it was too dark. Something told me I was in trouble and I just defended myself. The real surprise came when the guards came in and they tried to kill me as well. You see, I have to leave."

"The guards! Graedon should hear of this," retorted Ornelda.

"Hear, yes, but what can Father do in the meantime? He is ill and the guards answer to Lucio," replied the princess. "First we should help Brandyn escape and then bring the matter to Father's attention. The first place you should go," directed the princess, "is to Teresforte and Lord Barton. It is closer than Galles and the road is more direct. My uncle Barton will know what to do."

For now Brandyn was safe within the walls of that chamber so he was given a heavy blanket and he got some rest while Ornelda kept watch. One thing was certain. Brandon had to flee from Braemar Castle. Where should he go was the question.

Diabolical Plan

Lucio may have left the chambers of that room but he was convinced that Brandyn was in there. Where else could he be?

Lucio sensed his presence. Lucio summoned his young knights together with Sir Morden to lead them. For added assurance of his plan to work he would send Sir Chadryn, who came from Peregren, to attend the tournament games. Sir Chadryn had not departed from Peregren yet. Lucio had concocted a cruel and senseless, diabolical plot that would convince Graedon that he could not send his soldiers abroad. It was also a plot against Brandyn. Instead of killing him, he would destroy him alive. He would ruin his reputation so that his own family would be ashamed to receive him. The mention of his name would bring shame to the Wendover region and as for his girl, his motivation for living, he would take her away but not by force. What if she was to fall in love with another heroic, young knight who, say, saved her father from being killed in an enemy raid?

Lucio's thoughts were interrupted by the advent of his summoned party.

"There is no sign of him, my lord," reported Keveyn, who was tired.

"No matter, I know where he is," he replied sternly.

"Then let us get him and be done with him," snapped Franuch.

"You seem to have overlooked a certain detail," started Lucio. "Did you not notice that at the tournament games our young whelp sported a lady's kerchief?

They all were awoken by that notion. They remembered Brandyn taking out a lady's kerchief from his breast in the middle of the joust. They knew that Lucio had some demonic plan. Lucio would tell them his plan and they would execute it. They knew that this plan would be bad, real bad. They listened to Lucio as he unhatched this plan that was the dirtiest and most evil plot they would take part in to date. The plot involved mischief, deceit and murder. There would be the destruction of property and violence by design. Some innocent people would get hurt or even die. The young knights knew that it was wrong, but they were already guilty of smaller things that could cost them their place. So they said nothing and planned to do their master's bidding. Deeper and deeper they would sink.

Lucio would have chosen Marius for the task of winning over the girl who gave Brandyn her kerchief. Marius, however perfect for the role, just would not do. It was not because he lacked charm or fell short at the tournament games. The performance and exhibition of skills that Marius put forth at the games was excellent. Lucio had sensed that this young man had a conscience, was full of kindness and could not be counted on to do what had to be done. He did not even call him to the meeting. Marius was such a disappointment. Lucio had Keveyn in mind. Keveyn had no problem shutting off what little conscience he had to do anything that needed to be done. Keveyn also hated Brandyn almost as much as Lucio did. Unfortunately, he lacked the charm that would make him irresistible before a young, innocent maiden. April had received parental guidance.

With Morden in command, he dispatched them to make ready for his scheme, and they went without lament. This left him alone with Keveyn. He would now do the impossible. He would groom and teach Keveyn in the ways of the court and make him the perfect suitor for a young, impressionable maiden. The tailor was summoned to bring his fashioned garments and a barber to cut his hair. Foremost, Lucio's chamber maidens were called to fetch hot water so Keveyn could be given a bath. Lucio himself gave Keveyn the bath while feeding him instruction. Lucio demonstrated to him what to say and do to win over a maiden. It was Keveyn's hatred for Brandyn that made him a quick study.

East or West?

For Brandyn, the smart move would be to head for Teresforte as the princess had suggested. The trip was shorter than the one to Wendover and the weather could turn nasty without warning in late fall. Brandyn, with any luck, could even catch up with Barton's party of riders. He could then tell Barton his story and Barton would believe him and turn back. Barton did not trust Lucio and this story would not sit well with him. In the morning Princess Elayne would inform her father as well. Then this usurper of power would be brought to account in court before the people and their king. This was the smart move.

Brandyn's thoughts were occupied by April, his mother and father. Having to decide between Galles and Wendover turned into an internal struggle. Now here was another. Should he not go home to report of the good news that befell him despite the incident at the castle?

There were struggles everywhere, every day. Why should this struggle be any different or more important?

Brandyn's mind was made up; he just had to go home. At this point he was dreaming that he could even marry April and bring her to Galles with him.

In the morning Ornelda saw to it that Brandyn got a fine breakfast and had a chambermaid prepare a generous parcel of food for his trip. Ornelda, like the princess, was of the impression that Brandyn would head toward Teresforte and alert Lord Barton. Brandyn, however, had made his mind to go home to Wendover. Ornelda had insisted that the princess' plan was the smart thing to do. After listening to him talk about April though, it was understood that Brandyn was in love. The sentiment was enough to convince Elayne and Ornelda that going to Wendover would be the only place Brandyn could go. No one realized how truly serious the situation was. The princess admired Brandyn's open candour. She was not used to hearing men speak about another girl in her presence. Usually every young man she met, other than Jeremy, made it seem as though she was the only one alive. Elayne knew that she could trust Brandyn.

Brandyn believed that if he could make it home, the people in his village would rally to him because he became a knight. He also possessed the ring with the seal of Galles. Brandyn was Welledon's heir in Galles. Surely they would listen to him in Wendover. In the meanwhile, it was decided that Elayne would send word to both Barton and Welledon by a personal messenger. Then Elayne and Ornelda could alert Graedon in the morning. It was a reasonable plan, however, it would not be effective unless a trustworthy messenger was sent. Elayne was suspicious that if she tried to send out a dispatch, the contents of her message might be discovered. In the morning, matters got worse. Graedon did not get out of bed. It seemed as though the festivities took their toll on him. He was weak and tired. He could not focus on any thought without wanting to sleep and seemed to have aged immensely since retiring for bed the night before. It was as though he was under a spell.

Since the king's court adjourned, Lucio had been very busy. He had dispatched a party of knights and soldiers to the Wendover region with a hellish plot. A raid at night would be staged by Lucio's own men against Wendover. The same raid would then be put down by individuals that he chose to save the day. He was about to make new heroes from among his chosen. The people of Wendover would be made to believe that the raid came from Hammarsgard. Hammarsgard was home to people that lived in a rocky area to the northeast across the Mare Grigio. The people there had a history of raiding ships and established settlements that were scattered throughout the region. The people of Skaarsgard or Hammarsgard had the means, opportunity and a history of raiding Wendover. It would be easy to believe. The raid would happen at night so the people could not get a good view of the sea. The people would believe what they were told by the knights that Lucio sent to protect them.

Word had been sent to Tom, the farrier, to prepare Vento for the quick departure Brandyn would need to make. Tom complied and had Vento ready and waiting. Brandyn thanked Elayne and Ornelda for their support. He was given a sack with food provisions that Ornelda had arranged for. As he made his way through the castle across the great hall, Brandyn thought how strange the ease of his escape was becoming. Last night there were guards all over. It seemed that his path would not be crossed by one of them.

As he crossed the yard to the farrier's place of business, he saw Lucio looking down from one of the towers and he did not stir. He looked like a statue frozen in time. He did not move. Like a raven, he gave Brandyn a look that was condescending. It was as though he was allowing him to leave. The look worried Brandyn. He had come to know Lucio a lot better since the days of serving as Woodcroft's squire. The look worried him. After squaring his debt to Tom, the farrier, Brandyn mounted Vento and left Braemar for his ride to the east. He did not tell Tom anything. In this way, Tom could honestly say that he knew nothing if asked. He turned back to look at Lucio once more. Lucio wore a grin on his face. It was the same grin that he wore at the tournament. The look was troubling. He managed to get through the main castle gates without challenge. He then crossed the bridge to the road on the south side of Thermanden Bay. He was glad to be off and away, but there was something troublesome about the ease of his escape.

Ambitious Pursuit

In the chamber where Lucio was looking out from, he turned from the viewport and consulted with his mother about the "medication" for Graedon. There were many concoctions that Vanessa knew. She had long cared for injured men when she served under Sadar at Peregen. She had skill with roots and herbs, ales and spirits, and had experimented with the blood and other fluids of animals. If anyone had a means of perking up Graedon, it would be her. Then she could have easily concocted something to weaken him too. The truth is that she had already.

Vanessa advanced her son as far as she could at Peregren. She manipulated affairs between the arms makers and Federics. She instructed Lucio to give feigned expectations to the foreman of the blacksmiths. The unreasonable demands were seen as coming from Federics. Lucio pretended to take the blacksmiths' position and defend their rights. Gradually, Lucio developed a position of great influence with the foreman in charge of the blacksmiths there. The next step was Braemar, the king's castle. In order to help her son advance further, they moved to where the king was. Vanessa planned that, Graedon, the king, must be incapacitated. Graedon's Queen Annastasia had left him widowed with her sudden death a mere eight months prior. Perhaps she could bewitch him into falling in love with her. Then her son would have all the influence he required. Vanessa laughed at that notion, because she could get her way anytime she thought. What really appealed to her was for Lucio to marry Princess Elayne and produce a bloodline heir.

Since mid-summer Graedon had been drinking a strange tea that she brewed and which she drank herself on occasion. In small amounts the drink was invigorating. What Vanessa did not tell Graedon is that prolonged use of the tea from the lotumna tassesiae root would bring the adverse affect and leave him with a dependence on it and a slow, weary decline into death. In the meantime, Vanessa and Lucio could masquerade as a concerned physician and trusted confidant respectfully.

Prisoner in Her Own Castle

In the king's chamber, Sean, his trusted page, entered to tend to Graedon as he had done as a matter of habit and routine. He discovered his liege still in bed and not stirring. Graedon could not get up. He felt weak and tired and the mere utterance of speech or noise made him fall deeper into this sleep. In fact more increasingly Graedon had been tired lately, even after resting for the better part of the day. He had rested well to prepare for the Harvest Moon Fest tournament and games. He had managed to get through the grand event by virtue of sheer desire despite the loss of Annastasia, his wife and queen. The loss of the queen had taken the entire kingdom by surprise. Her Majesty was in perfect health, or so it was believed that she was. Then one winter morning she lay motionless in her bed. The loss was sudden and great for the king, but he made an effort to attend the function. It was gratifying to a monarch that his people were happy with their portion of comfort. He was glad he attended. It gave him the strength to see the festivities through. Today, however, his condition was worse. Perhaps it was the added scuffle of the previous night.

Elayne entered the royal chamber. She wanted to inform her father about what had happened to Brandyn last night in the castle. She was surprised to learn that her father was not up. This was unusual because he managed to get up no matter what ailed him before. The chamber maiden brought in the Lotuma tea that had become a common drink for the king. She placed the tray on the table and stepped back. There was no need to pour out. At that instance Lucio entered the outer chamber with another servant who carried a tray with some bread and red wine, as a matter of routine. Lucio was anxious about getting the king's signature on the letters he had fashioned. He had already arranged a delegation as discussed the night before. Now all he needed was the king's seal and hand.

With the king too ill to get up, he quickly sent a page to summon his mother to come. With the page gone, Elayne ran out to summon Harpe, the king's personal physician. She did not trust Vanessa or Lucio for that matter. With Elayne gone, Lucio removed Graedon's ring with the seal of Rothaynen. He went to the king's desk and forged his hand with a quill. These were the letters for the emissaries, Tonio and Arno. Graedon had intended to write the letters himself but could not do so know. Since Lucio knew the essence of the content, he wrote the letters. Lucio had the letters with him all folded politely. He took the letters and melted wax on the seam of each. There with Graedon's ring, he stamped the cooling hot wax with the seal of Rothaynen. He hid the letters on his person and left the tray on the king's desk. Lucio had just turned to return the ring to the king's finger when he heard someone coming. He immediately hid the ring to discover that it was only Vanessa who stepped into the chamber, but she was followed by Elayne and Harpe.

Vanessa looked stunningly beautiful for an early riser after a late night. Harpe began to examine His Majesty. Having noted that the servant brought tea, Vanessa objected to the king having lotumna tea in his condition. She had accurately assessed his condition. However, she cited that the grief over the passing of the queen was the cause. After all, she noted, that he was fine just yesterday at the knighting ceremony.

"I am afraid that our king is mourning the passing of his wife, the queen," she said, convincing herself as though it were fact. Harpe agreed as there was no other reason for the king to be weak. Vanessa recommended pea soup, bread, cheese and tomato with garden spices and water for a drink. She also suggested the king be taken outside into the fresh air and was appalled at the lack of cleanliness in his chamber. The servants were not thrilled with her comments. Harpe could only agree with Vanessa's suggestions and assured Elayne that her father would be fine. Harpe assured Elayne that he would check in on Graedon later. All of Vanessa's suggestions were good, especially having Graedon withdraw from the drinking of lotumna tea. Vanessa knew, however, that Graedon had become addicted to it. Graedon would throw a fit over his dependence and need for the tea. He would be needing and wanting more and more of the strange brew until it lead him to death.

With her father incapacitated, Elayne was frightened. There would be no time to show fear now. *I will be frightened later,* she thought. Elayne could not show Lucio or Vanessa that she suspected anything. Lucio was certain that she knew about Brandyn's whereabouts the night before, but he pretended that he did not. Vanessa sensed her distress over her father and spoke some comforting words to her. "Do not be afraid, your royal father will be fine in no time." Vanessa approached the princess with the intention of placing her arm around her. However, in that instance, Elayne walked toward her father's bedside and kneeled before him instead. She took her father's hand and started to say a prayer silently. She noticed that the ring with the seal of Rothaynen was missing off her father's hand. Graedon had never removed the ring from his finger.

"Where is my father's ring?" she inquired.

"Your father was writing letters last evening. Perhaps it is on his desk," replied Lucio as he walked over to the desk. When he arrived there, Lucio took the ring from his garment and placed it on the desk.

"There it is," noted Lucio.

Elayne stood up and walked over to the desk. She saw the ring and picked it up. She noticed that the quill her father used to write with was still wet with fresh ink. The smell gave it away, as did the scent of burning wax. The princess could do nothing about it now. She walked over to her father with the ring and placed it on his finger.

After that she left her father in the hands of Vanessa and Lucio and went to find Ornelda. Elayne was sure that the ring with the seal of Rothaynen was on her father's finger when she first entered the room that morning. She knew that her father never removed it. What Elayne did not realize was that her father's ailment was prolonged by the consumption of the very tea that Vanessa forbade Graedon to take. Vanessa appeared quite concerned and capable with nursing Graedon. Elayne feared she had to inform Barton and Welledon sooner than later but who could she depend on?

Ornelda was the only person whose loyalty she could fully trust. She knew the servants well, but the allegiance of some could be bought with silver. If Elayne sent Ornelda alone with the correspondence however, then who could she trust to be with her in the castle?

She and Ornelda could leave together, but then she would leave her father in unfriendly hands.

Although she was the princess and this was her father's castle, she was a prisoner.

When she found her, Elayne brought Ornelda to her chamber to discuss the matter. What happened to Brandyn the previous night was not common or good. Barton would be the quickest to inform since Teresforte was directly to the west. From there Barton would return to Braemar with his forces. Elayne grabbed her plume, ink and a scroll to write her message on. Ornelda was helpful in reminding her of the details, but she stressed that Elayne should be brief. They decided that one of the king's pages should be trusted to go. They were sure that they could trust Sean. Even if he was noticed as missing, Elayne would admit that she summoned him to send word to Lord Barton about her father's illness. She could ask Lucio to write the message but in turn secretly give Sean one of her own.

Lucio had prepared a party of diplomats and knights to escort Arno to Wendover and then board a Craigroyston ship that would take the delegation to Leems. Lucio had delayed the diplomats departure as long as he could so the disaster he sent upon Wendover could be carried out well before this delegation arrived. Not only would they act as witnesses to the attack on Wendover, but Lucio could now advise Graedon that their forces would be needed on the homeland to defend his people. At this time Rothaynen could not venture out to help Leems, but Lucio could try his diplomatic approach. As Lucio had suggested, a generous supply of wheat flour was gathered to be sent as tribute to Karnivron. Barton and Welledon were incensed at this. "Charity was alright, but tribute, never!" Senus, the very tax collector who collected it for the king's granaries, was sent on the diplomatic errand to Karnivron. If Lucio could make an agreement with Karnivron, he would gladly sacrifice Leems to him to keep Rothaynen free, free for himself.

Treachery

At the Wendover Lowlands, the party of knights and soldiers that Lucio had dispatched with the diabolical plan arrived. They brought with them relics of previous battles with Agreggian tribes who raided Wendover in the past. They planted these weapons and items of dress to leave evidence of their presence. A group of knights rode onto the countryside to warn the farmers and call for women and children to go to the Wendover Tavern for safety. Then, one farm at a time, like a harvest, they set fires and scared off the farmers. They even killed the farmers who tried to defend their home and land.

In the case of the Cranston homestead, a party of knights and soldiers arrived to help Cranston. Cranston complied and sent Ellen, April and Courtenay away to the tavern for safety. Sure enough, there was a fire that started in the barn. Cranston ran over to the barn with his sword and knife before anyone else could react. Cranston confronted a large, dirty man he saw going into the barn. It was Franuch. He fought fiercely with him. Minor wounds were exchanged. Finally, Cranston subdued Franuch who lay on his back on the ground dead, just as Keveyn arrived.

"I sure got this one!" he acclaimed

Keveyn replied, "You sure did." The unsuspecting Cranston was stabbed by Keveyn's sword. Cranston was in shock and could not react. He never expected that a king's knight would turn on him. It was too late, though. Cranston recognized the treachery but could do nothing. Cranston lay in front of the barn with his face down in the mud. He had wanted to save the barn from being burned. While he lay dying from the mortal wound, he could hear the fire in the barn increase in its voracity.

Unknown to them both was the presence of Courtenay, who witnessed the whole affair. Courtenay had forgotten her doll in the barn and just had to go back to retrieve it. In all that ensued, Courtenay saw the large man enter the barn with the torch. Out of fear and curiosity, she hid silently. When he lit the straw on fire she was going to dash out the barn's side door but her father had arrived. Courtenay witnessed her father fight bravely to defend their home. It was when she saw her father stabbed by someone that he trusted, that she gasped. Her gasp alerted Dermon, a duteous soldier who followed Keveyn to the barn. Courtenay was so frightened she wanted to run away, but she wanted to run to her father's side too. When Courtenay recovered her composure, she ducked down and carefully crawled across the barn floor. She opened the side door and darted for safety. As careful as she was, Dermon was listening and saw her as she got up to run out the doorway to the side of the barn.

"Look, company," he blurted out.

They all converged out the very doorway that Courtenay departed out of. The other wicked men on horseback saw her and gave chase. Courtenay fainted from the fatigue, heartache and fear.

"Let's kill her and be done with it," offered Dermon, who was proud of his discovery. Dermon felt he had saved the day.

"No!" retorted Morden.

"She may have seen too much," worried Keveyn.

"She witnessed combat in the dark. She saw her father killed during a raid. Who cares what she saw?" Morden thought aloud. "She is the sister of the maiden who gave Brandyn the kerchief. I have a better plan."

Although she was unconscious and unaware of the planned treachery, she was quite sure of the person who had stabbed her father. She would never forget that face. If anyone else had come to her comfort, she would believe their story. However, it was Keveyn, the same Keveyn, who climbed down off his horse and picked her up like a dutiful knight. She could not speak or move with fear. The party rode off to the Wendover tavern while the home fires burned.

At the tavern, where many of the women and young children had come for shelter and safety, there was great anxiety. They wondered whether the enemy had been stopped and who was hurt.

The mock attack resulted in the murder of many farmers and their sons who thought they were defending their families and homesteads in earnest against an enemy from Hammarsgard. In truth, they were fighting an enemy, but not from Hammarsgard. The people from Hammarsgard had been conspicuously absent from attacks on Wendover that fall. What Lucio did not know was two key items that would not support his story. First, Craigroyston established trade with Skaarsgard so they no longer raided. Second, the Huysnten invasion force that failed at Wendover started sailing east for home. Since they did not want to disappoint their king and arrive home empty-handed, they sailed northeast for Hammarsgard. The Huynsten invader overwhelmed the settlement at Haagens in Hammarsgard and laid waste to the homes and annihilated its people. The settlement at Haagens was an Arsgardian tribe and relations with the people of Skaarsgard.

Morden had publicly ordered that "their enemies dead bodies be gathered that very night and be cast into the sea from whence they came." Although people witnessed the soldiers riding out for this task, there were no "enemy bodies," not from Skaarsgard or Hammarsgard anyway. It just looked good when upon their return, Morden declared aloud in the tavern, that the enemy was driven back into the sea. The fallen soldiers involved in the attack were merely stripped of their Hammarsgard regalia, which was collected as evidence. Although these were the soldiers that died at the hands of the Wendover farmers who were defending their homes, these soldiers now served as heroes. These traitors were brought to Wendover to receive an honorable funeral as defenders of the king's people.

Daring Insolence

It was recommended that the farms people stay the night at the tavern on the chance there might still be skirmishes. The women were very anxious to learn of their loved ones that they left behind to defend their farms. Some of the men returned to their families at the tavern and reported that their farms were not attacked. Others who waited were not encouraged as time passed and no word came. Malcolm had left his tavern to join his neighbours in the struggle and rode his horse high atop the escarpment to spy on the sea. If there were raiders, they would come from the sea. He could see their movements and report to the knights. Although there was cloud cover, and it was misty, the moon did appear enough for him to see the open sea. There was no evidence of any ship on the high seas. There was just the diplomatic ship from Craigroyston at the harbour. Surely if there were trouble that ship would have responded. The ship had been there a few days to drop off the emissaries so they could speak to Graedon's court. Perhaps the raiders were dropped off farther up the shoreline. He rode up the coast and again he saw no ship. Had the ships abandoned their raiders?

He thought that was hardly the case. There had been some mistake and he would inform the first set of fighting men he saw.

At the tavern, Eileen and April were anxious. Quite some time had passed and they had yet to see Courtenay. She had ran back to get her doll and had not yet returned. At that time a group of knights entered the tavern. One of them was carrying a little girl. The little girl was Courtenay. The knight was upset that he had not been able to save the girl's father. "If only we had arrived earlier, we may have saved the brave fighting man," Keveyn said in a regretful manner.

Eileen gasped and put both her hands over her mouth. She removed them to ask, "Where is my husband?"

She could not hold back her tears as April comforted her. They had been through raids before but Cranston was a tough fighting man. He always came through.

April started to tear up in disbelief. She asked, "Is Courtenay dead too?"

At that moment Kevyn understood why Brandyn would be taken with this young maiden they called April.

"This young lady is not dead but in shock," reported Keveyn.

The only reason she was alive was that Morden opposed killing her. That in itself was odd, but it had been Dermon's suggestion to kill her. Since he had spoken out of turn, Morden chose to spare her. Eileen took Courtenay in her arms and held her close. Meaghan brought a pitcher of water and poured some in a small goblet for her. Hearing the familiar voice of her mother and April who took her hand, Courtenay slowly regained some consciousness. She wanted to tell her mother everything. It was like a bad dream.

"Look," encouraged Eileen, "she has awoken."

Eileen took the water and gave it up to Courtenay to drink. As she drank she saw Keveyn, Morden, Dermon and the other traitors gathered around the tavern as though they had done no wrong and were heroes. A look of horror overtook her and she tried to speak but could not.

"Do not be afraid," comforted April. "These men brought you to us."

Courtenay's eyes did not leave the men who had brought her there. Her mother noticed her fear of the strangers and she told her, "Do not be afraid. These are the brave men who saved you."

Courtenay was confused and dumbfounded.

Her mother said, "This was the good knight who brought you here," as she indicated Keveyn.

Keveyn appeared empathetic. "My name is Keveyn. You have nothing to fear now, young lady. You are with your mother and sister now."

Keveyn realized his presence disturbed her and he wanted it that way. He backed off to make it look like he was considerate and understanding of her situation. "Perhaps my appearance and manner are frightening your daughter," he said humbly as he withdrew. "My apology."

"No. Keveyn, with all the loss we incurred this night, we are grateful to you all. It was you that returned our daughter."

"What was she doing there?" Keveyn questioned to create small talk. "Every young maiden was to come to the town for safety."

Lucio's training was yielding dividends. Speaking slowly and calmly, Keveyn portrayed empathy and concern. The story was accepted and there was no suspicion about the raid. What is more is that he struck up a conversation. Conversation was of no purpose to Keveyn before. To him people were implements to be used. When he previously wanted something he just took it. He was not a man of words. Now he was enjoying himself as the very people he deceived were thanking and welcoming him and making conversation.

Keveyn had killed Cranston callously after Cranston, in self-defence, apprehended and slew the traitor. Franuch, who had been the traitor, would be transported back to Solce and receive a hero's burial and be placed in a grave of honour. Although Franuch's death angered Keveyn, his thoughts were not on grieving. Keveyn delighted in this game of deceit. He wondered how long it would take before he could make April fall for him. He envisioned taking her for himself so she would serve him, willingly. With this new facade of his, he could easily accomplish this.

Morden took delight in the situation. His men were heroes and his master's bidding was done. "Keveyn," he recommended, "perhaps you and a few men should accompany these ladies to their home and stay on until they no longer require your protection."

"If you say so, sir," Keveyn replied, giving the impression he was submissive and dutiful to the commands of an elder knight.

Eileen could not speak to accept or reject the notion. She was unaware of what had transpired. Her only thought was the disbelief that Cranston was dead. Perhaps if they went home they would see him. April had practical thoughts. To return unaccompanied, without a fighting man to defend them should they meet with trouble, seemed unpractical. Courtenay had retreated into sleep and could not communicate the horror she witnessed. So on Morden's command, a party of soldiers, led by his brave Keveyn, would accompany the family of the man that he had murdered. He was to act as their protector, after all, he had rescued and delivered Courtenay safe and sound. Keveyn had not eaten and asked if he could do so before they departed for the Cranston homestead. How could anyone deny a young hero a meal?

The Homecoming

It was at about this time that Brandyn arrived at the west gate of the Wendover Lowlands. Although it was dark you could still see the cut straw that lay on the rolling fields, but the sweet smell in the air was absent. The moonlight, cut grass and brisk night air made a nice picture if it were not for the smell of smoke. He would learn that the home fires had burned. He would naturally cross Cranston's homestead on his route home to the tavern. The rising smoke from the burnt-out barn was an indicator of what had happened there. He was concerned. April was not there. Cranston's family was not there. There had been a raid. He rode on toward the barn and discovered Cranston, face down in the dirt. He noticed that his blood congealed around the fatal wound he had received. There was a trail of dirt behind him. He must have been wounded trying to save his barn and then crawled away to avoid burning to death. Brandyn was in utter shock. He could not believe it. This man was Cranston, April's father. He loved this man like his own father. Now he lay dead. Where was the rest of his family, and where was April?

Brandyn dismounted his horse and pulled Cranston's face out of the mud. He lay Cranston's head up against some thick grass for support but that would not comfort the dead man.

On his journey to the tavern, he wondered about his own family. As he approached he could see evidence of ill deeds. He saw the faint light of the tavern from a distance. He anticipated the warmth of that light. He anticipated the warmth that meant he was home. He anticipated the warmth that came from being reunited with his family. He would be robbed of that secure feeling when he learned that Morden and a party of knights were stationed there. In measures of war they were, by royal decree, in charge over the town and its people. The Wendover Tavern was the ideal place for a command post.

Earlier that evening, Morden had sent a party out to secure Plenitude Church and collect the pastor to come to the safety of the tavern. That was the order that everyone in the tavern heard. A knight named Sir Chadryn and some soldiers were dispatched. Chadryn's real orders were to take care of unfinished work from the past. His orders were to kill the pastor and set the church on fire. Since they were gone so long, two soldiers were sent to check up on them at the church.

Brandyn entered the tavern. Andrea and Meaghan were inside anxiously waiting attentively for news about Malcolm. They were happy to see Brandyn. The first thing Brandyn learned was that his father had rode out but not returned from his errand to alert the farmers about the raid. Malcolm was told that there was a raid. The presence of Graedon's knights and army at Wendover led him to believe it. So off he rode to warn his neigbours about the pillagers. Malcolm had still not returned. Brandyn saw Eileen, Courtenay, April and other women and children of the community. They all looked at each other but no one said a word. There was a thick silence. They were all anxious.

In the midst of anticipating bad news, Brandyn gained hope and strength in just seeing that his mother and sister and April were alright. April saw him too but they could not engage in conversation. Andrea was so happy to see her son that after her surprise at seeing him, she directly went to him. She threw her arms around him. Andrea said, "Thank God you are safe, but I am very worried about your father. He rode out to the top of the Wendover escarpment and has not yet returned."

It was then that Brandyn got an awful feeling about his father. Malcolm had often rode to the Wendover escarpment to scout where invaders were headed. He would learn of their movements and numbers. He warned his neighbours and alerted the soldiers. He always returned from these errands. He looked at Meaghan for a moment and then turned toward April. She saw him too. Before Brandyn could walk over and greet the girl he longed to see, he was attacked verbally by Morden.

"You are late,"chided Morden with hostility. "What good are you now? You were supposed to join us in coming to the defence of Wendover's people, instead you spent the night in the castle with the princess."

"I did not receive any orders—"

"Of course not, you were with the princess. Do you deny it?"

"No, I do not, but how do you know?"

"What use are you now?" Morden was conveying that Brandyn might have made a difference had he shown up. April was displeased with hearing about the princess, let alone not showing up to save their people. Her own father was killed.

"The death of many of the king's subjects took place at the hands of pirates from Hammarsgard this night. The rest of us risked our lives but the new Archduke of Galleysia was busy climbing ahead socially."

Brandyn did not know where to begin defending himself. The shock of the raid had been enough.

Andrea intervened, "If you have quite finished, I have not heard from my son."

"Naturally, you speak to him," Morden said with disgust. "The rest of us need to retire from this ordeal."

At that moment, the messenger that was sent to fetch over Pastor Mattews had alarming news. Upon their return from Plenitude Church, the soldier had his report.

"What took so long?"asked Morden.

"There was smoke in the church. Someone tried to set the tapestries on fire. We pulled the smoking tapestries into the church yard and put out the cinders. They were mostly wet and were only smoking. There is little damage done to them."

Morden could not care less about the "tapestries" or the church for that matter. "Where is Chadryn?!" he questioned firmly. "Make it quick!"

"Sir Chadryn is lying dead in the church garden. His soldiers are slain. The church is empty and there is no sign of Pastor Mattews."

The report surprised Morden. He thought, *how could a big man like Chadryn be dead? He was a skilled assassin that was given the simple task of killing a preacher. There were no raiders. They were the raiders! What about Pastor Mattews? Maybe a group of local people ambushed the men?*

After a brief moment for thought Morden ordered, "Ferns, take a group of soldiers to secure the church in case the raiders attempt to set fire to it again."

The rest of the knights in his service took their leave in the tavern's upstairs rooms to gain much needed rest. In the camp of soldiers, word was given to be alert. It was a twist of fate that they, the perpetrators, had to be alert. The odd turn of events in the church gave them something to worry about. It had been a long, tiring night for them as they had worked Lucio's treacherous plan. The other soldiers that were present returned to their camp site and posted more watches to guard the sleeping men. They all took their leave, departing as though the entire situation was the fault of Brandyn. It was as if they had been the injured party.

Morden concluded his berating of Brandyn by ignoring him. He did let him know that Cranston's family would be escorted back to their home. "Keveyn," he called softly, "you had better get on your way with the escort."

At that point, Brandyn witnessed Eileen and April get up and make their way to the tavern door. Keveyn picked up and carried

Courtenay in his arms. They would not even look in his direction except for April.

"Please allow me to help," Brandyn appealed to Eileen.

"Your place is here with your mother and sister," she replied to him. Eileen was hurt over the loss of her husband. She would believe anything she heard now. She would believe that Brandyn could have made a difference. It was what Morden said, and he was in charge. Eileen turned away from Brandyn and toward Keveyn, who would escort them home. Her family followed Keveyn out of the tavern.

Brandyn felt a pain in his heart and a numbness came over his lips. With all that had ensued, Brandyn was portrayed as careless, self-serving and irresponsible. He was not given orders. What orders had he been given?

He had to flee from Braemar after an assassination attempt on his own life. The whole matter stunned him.

The entire Wendover Lowlands was stunned at the tragedy that befell them. Many husbands and sons had died that night. More accurately, they were murdered for a personal vendetta. The word about Brandyn being hassled by Morden at the tavern would get out quickly. It would be as though the entire tragedy was Brandyn's fault. He would have made all the difference and his absence was to blame.

Andrea and Meaghan were taken by the shock of the attack, the death of Cranston and the fact that Malcolm had not returned. The berating that her son had received was not encouraging. Still, they gave him the benefit of the doubt. "You two had better get some rest. You look like you have not slept in days," Brandyn told them.

Andrea and Meaghan would not retire for the night, as they did not feel safe or trust Morden's company of knights who occupied the tavern rooms. How could they sleep now with all they heard about Brandyn?

"Sleep?" questioned Meaghan, "with father still absent, that fancy ring on your finger, news of a princess and these knights turning on you?"

Brandyn explained, "I did well at the tournament, but it was Lord Welledon who gave me the ring with the seal of Galles."

"Were you really with the princess last night?"

"Indeed I was," he stated, as Meaghan looked surprised. "I was fortunate enough to be invited into her chambers while escaping from assassins that tried to kill me in my room," Brandyn added. "There were no orders for me to accompany Morden to Wendover. Would I not jump at the chance to come home? I did not know they were leaving to protect Wendover. How did they know there would be a raid?"

"Why are there assassins after you?" Meaghan questioned in distress with hearing this news.

"It is Lucio," replied Brandyn. "He tried to kill Lord Barton so I flung a plate at his wrist. Everything was supposed to have calmed down, but that same night two assassins tried to kill me in my sleep. After I got away from them, the guards tried to kill me. It was Lucio's will, his plan. Just like the death of Woodcroft, it was planned by Lucio. I just know it."

Meaghan was still sensitive about losing Woodcroft, for they were truly in love. She did not know what to make of this accusation.

"We are worried about Malcolm and now we are worried about you," said Andrea.

"How does the princess fit into the story?" asked Meaghan.

"When I was making my escape down the corridor of the castle, I realized I was trapped. I climbed the stone walls up to the beams and avoided one search party. After they left I climbed down. Princess Elayne had opened her chamber door and was standing before me. She and her lady, Ornelda, hid me from the pursuit."

"There was no personal bond between you and the princess then?" asked Andrea.

"Other than her saving my life, no."

"April looked rather surprised when she heard that you had spent the night with the princess," she reminded him.

"How could I get in to see the princess?" he asked.

"You are the one with that fancy ring," she replied.

"Why did Keveyn get picked to escort Cranston's family home?" he asked with concern.

"The other knights seemed to lack refinement. He was the most like a knight should be."

"Keveyn?" he questioned incredulously.

"He saved Courtenay from sure death when he rescued her. Now he is returning to Cranston's stead to help them get readjusted," recounted his mother.

"He could not care less about anybody but himself," replied Brandyn.

"Do I sense a note of jealousy?" questioned his sister.

"You just do not know him or Morden. Morden and Keveyn are Lucio's puppets. The tough, mean kind. That Morden infuriates me. He is self-serving, selfish and selective. They all are. This is a plot. It is a plot to discredit me. Lucio is merciless. When he hates someone, he really knows how to hate."

The feeling of anger, disgust and disbelief occupied Brandyn's mind. He could think of no one but April. From the moment he returned to Wendover, he could not make sense of what had happened: what evil had taken over. Why was Keveyn with Cranston's family and not him? "Will you allow me to ride out there?"appealed Brandyn.

"At this time?" questioned his mother. "I would rather you stay here with me and your sister. There are all those men about us. If what you are saying is true—"

"Mother, I have got to talk to April," he interrupted.

Meaghan understood him straight away. She grasped what it was that was going on.

"Go," she told her brother, "I know she means everything to you. I do not want to see you lose her. Go and bring them all back here. We will be fine until you get back."

With those words he went out. Brandyn was quick to mount Vento and race for Cranston's homestead in west Wendover.

Assumptions

On the way to escorting Cranston's family to their home, Keveyn kept quiet. He answered any questions in short sentences so as to provoke more questions. Eileen had a heavy heart over the death of her husband and was concerned over Courtenay, who was still in deep shock. She could not speak nor did she hear what was being said. It was April who was curious about Brandyn and the princess. "Have you met the princess?" she asked Keveyn.

"She was present at the tournament games."

"Did the princess present the champions with a token?"

"No, King Graedon himself did that."

April wanted to come out and ask him, "Just how did Brandyn end up spending the night with the princess?" Instead she tried to come up with more questions in a roundabout way. "Was there a celebration after the contest?"

"Yes," replied Keveyn.

"Was there dancing?"

"Yes," replied Keveyn.

"Did you get to dance with the princess?"

"No," replied Keveyn, "but other knights did. In fact, I think she rather liked a certain one." Keveyn knew that the princess danced with Jeremy, but April would think he was referring to Brandyn. He was not responsible for her assumption. Her heart, already heavy with the loss of her father, was now broken. Brandyn had told her that he loved her. She had given him the only linen kerchief she owned. He was just like any other boy who would love whomever he was with in the moment, she thought. She was silent for the rest of the trip. Keveyn kept riding proper and straight. He did not speak a word for the rest of the trip either. He was just doing his duty. Keveyn basked in what he had just done.

When they arrived at the Cranston homestead, they saw the barn had burned down. The air smelled of smoke. As they got closer, they saw the body of Cranston lying face up. Earlier, Brandyn had pulled him out of the mud. The sight was disturbing to Eileen and April. Keveyn dismounted his horse and removed his cape. He then draped it over Cranston. Keveyn returned to help Eileen with getting Courtenay in the house. April sat down beside her father. They returned to collect Cranston. Eileen would bathe him in preparation for the burial tomorrow. The horses would have to be tended and watered so Eileen asked April to do so. Keveyn gave Eileen a hand with getting Cranston into the house. She started to build a fire to warm up the home. With Cranston in the house, Keveyn now had all the time in the world to talk to April while she tended the horses.

"You have not said much since the early part of the journey," Keveyn noted.

"There is not much to say," replied April.

"I really am sorry about your father. He was a good man who fought bravely. It is just that we were overrun. He was a brave man." He paused. "I truly am sorry."

"Did you see him die?" asked April.

"Yes," Keveyn said, saying little.

One Final Assassination

Back at the tavern, Morden had not really retired for the night. He did not sleep. After hearing Brandyn's plan to ride out to Cranston's farm, he had an idea. Moments after Brandyn left the Wendover Tavern, Morden dispatched three men, disguised as raiders, who were good with knives. He sent them after Brandyn. In the morning it would look like Brandyn met his end at the hands of raiders from Hammarsgard just like the others. Morden delighted in this plot and only marvelled at how easily everything was falling into place. He thought about how Lucio would be pleased to hear that Brandyn was killed like a lamb at the slaughter. His interests now turned toward Meaghan.

Brandyn was already half dead but not from the lack of sleep or the ride to Wendover. Brandyn could not bear to see April with another man, especially Keveyn, who, like Lucio, did not care for anyone but himself. Brandyn's love for April was consuming him. This love had the power to override his fatigue yet at the same time, it left him fatigued in a worse manner. He could not imagine what life would be like without April. She was the only girl that he thought of the entire trip to Braemar, during the tournament and the trip back to Wendover.

There came upon him an awful thought. He imagined April giving herself to Keveyn and a rush of desire filled his veins with anger and strength. Not much later the same thought of April giving herself to Keveyn weakened him worse than before. He could not sense anything but what his mind concocted. It was all bad; he imagined the worst.

Somehow Brandyn managed to hear the trampling hooves of horses not far behind him. He turned to see who it might be at this late hour. He surmised that with that menacing speed there may be danger. Brandyn rode off the road toward the forest fence to see if they followed, and they did without reservation. Brandyn thought he might have to lose them in the forest. It was hard to see in the forest path so he had to slow down. The riders drew closer. At an instance a knife was thrown at him that caught his left arm. It made him lose control over Vento. Having sensed this, Vento knew how to keep his master in the saddle. The pain of the knife wound, however, and his fatigue were too much. Brandyn collapsed forward on the mane of his horse. The assassins relented in their charge as they came closer to their wounded victim. They surrounded him. Vento could do nothing. One dismounted and approached the horse. They were about to finish Brandyn when they too were surprised by arrows that pierced them. It seemed that the arrows came from the road ahead.

It was Tonio and Arno, the emissaries from Craigroyston and Leems respectively. An entourage from Braemar was escorting them to the ship anchored in the harbor at Wendover. The emissaries departure had been deliberately stalled by Lucio to allow the fake raid on Wendover to take place. It was thought that by the time they rode through Wendover, the mock raid would be over. Tonio and Arno would arrive in time to witness the threat to Graedon's people in Wendover from the Arsgardian tribes. Ironically, Senus' men shot down the assassins sent by Morden.

Senus declared, "Do you see what the people have to endure from these savages from Hammarsgard?"

Senus himself realized that the faces on the assassins were familiar. The costumes were authentic, yet they surprised Tonio. Tonio was aware that King Jonquis had an agreement with both the people of Skaarsgard and Hammarsgard. "There is an agreement between the Arsgardian tribes and Craigroyston that there will be no more raids," Tonio quietly reminded Arno. It is peculiar that the Arsgardian tribes would raid and risk their lives when they could trade. Tonio questioned in his mind, *if they were from Hammarsgard, what were they doing so deep into the land?* This place was in west Wendover and far from the sea. Senus remained silent and now contemplated having to kill the emissaries. Arno thought that he should play dumb to the observations.

"Tonio, there are always self-serving pirates who do not recognize diplomacy," offered Arno. Tonio looked on in agreement. For the moment Senus was satisfied that the two emissaries did not suspect foul play.

"We had better tend to Graedon's brave knight," suggested Arno, as his ruse worked.

Arno called for his servant to tend to Graedon's knight who was ambushed.

"My Lord, he is wounded," called back an escort of Arno.

"He is not moving; is it serious?" asked Arno.

"No, he appears to be exhausted though," was the reply.

Arno dismounted his horse and approached the wounded knight. He recognized him at an instance. Who could forget the face of the young knight who saved Lord Barton at Graedon's court a few nights before?

Senus also saw who it was. He realized that it was his soldiers' intervention that saved this life.

As the attendant looked after the knife wound in Brandyn's left shoulder, Tonio and Arno examined the dead assassins. The garb would lend itself to saying they were from Skaarsgard or Hammarsgard. The faces and hair, however, did not match the ruggedness of a warrior from that region. The Arsgard warriors had long, strawberry blond hair with beards and moustaches. In fact, one man's face looked familiar. Arno remembered the face from the tournament games at Braemar Castle. Tonio and Arno said nothing.

Since Arno and Tonio were accompanied by Senus and an armed escort of King Graedon, they said nothing. They did not share their thoughts with Senus, as they remembered how unruly matters got at court a few days earlier. Both Tonio and Arno were still on Graedon's domain yet they too did not know who to trust. They would all ride on to the harbor and board the Craigroyston ship. From there Graedon's delegation would be sailed to Leems as planned. Arno, however, would also take an extra passenger and his horse. He sensed that this was the only way to save the young knight's life.

Brandyn was unconscious but not solely from the wound. It was due to fatigue and mainly heartache. He had lost some blood, but Arno's servant washed and bandaged the wound. Brandyn was put on his horse, Vento, and taken across Wendover directly to the ship that awaited Tonio, Arno and their party. Brandyn's life was saved, but his plans to see and rescue April would not happen this day. Word of his whereabouts would not make its way to his mother and sister at Wendover, and he did not learn of his father's fate either.

Far and Away

When Brandyn regained consciousness, he was on a large ship with sails that flew the colours of Craigroyston. The ram and anchor on the flags were identifying symbols. The weapons and armed men of the seafaring vessel immediately told that you were on a naval warship. As he looked out he could see the rolling waves of the grey sea with white foam appearing wherever the vessel disturbed the water. It was cold and windy. He looked back and could not see the escarpment that was familiar to him. Brandyn concluded that his destiny was not in his hands anymore. Arno cared for him and his wound. Brandyn was laid to rest in a cabin on the vessel. Arno realized that Brandyn had been in danger since he performed the bold rescue at court. Arno did not share his thoughts with Senus, whom Lucio had chosen to send.

In his cabin Brandyn could not sleep; his thoughts were about April. It was after all his guests were assigned quarters that Arno entered Brandyn's cabin and asked the youth, "Have you something to declare?"

Brandyn decided that he had no choice but to trust Arno. He relayed to him everything that happened to him since the evening of Graedon's court. Arno told Brandyn that after Graedon's diplomats were sailed to Leems, Brandyn could sail back to Wendover. Wendover was on the way back to Craigroyston, which was Tonio's destination. After reporting to Henrickard, Arno might have to sail with Tonio on a new mission. Arno could sense that Brandyn was of good character and genuine so he proposed a plan. Arno's plan called for Brandyn to accompany Senus to Leems and spy on him. "You could do your king a great service if you were to follow Senus when he speaks to Karnivron and learn his plans. There is not a knight among them. You could easily join them."

"That would be treason to spy on my king's diplomat," he justly lamented.

"Someone tried to kill you at the castle. You were ambushed on the road," listed Arno.

"Raiders from Skaarsgard," explained Brandyn.

"No,"Arno stated firmly.

"Raiders from Hammarsgard?" questioned Brandyn.

"Performers," stated Arno.

"Performers?" Brandyn repeated.

"Performers. The sailors reported to Tonio that no other ship came near to the Wendover harbor that entire evening nor that night. Those raiders were from among the king's own people, his own soldiers perhaps. One of the assassins that we subdued had a familiar face. I recognized him from the tournament at Braemar. They were sent to kill you. What about the chamber incident in the castle that you told me about?"

Brandyn did not want to believe it, but it was true. It explained everything.

"I will get word to your family that you are safe. I will inform them that you were assigned to a diplomatic mission. That should leave them at ease over you," Arno continued. "In the meantime you can learn what takes place at the meetings between Senus and Karnivron. Then we may learn what the plans of Graedon's advisor, Lucio, truly are."

"You are worried about Leems,"Brandyn realized.

"I am very concerned about Leems, your people and those of Craigroyston. If Senus betrays us and strikes up an accord of nonaggression—" Arno stopped himself and rephrased, "if Senus makes a pledge with Karnivron not to help Leems, then by itself Leems is surely doomed. After Leems falls into the hands of Karnivron, he will get strong using Leems resources. Then, in due time, they will attack Graedon's kingdom and Jonquis' kingdom."

"Why would they do that?" inquired Brandyn.

"Your Wendover region is constantly raided for the wheat and grains that you grow. Those grains make bread. Bread feeds people. People who are fed are easier to oversee. So why should they risk losing warriors in raiding Wendover when they could conquer and rule it?"

Brandyn remembered the failed Huynsten invasion. He realized that Arno was right, this mission was his duty. It was Lucio who had tried to kill him. Lucio surely killed Woodcroft as though it was he that ran his sword through him on the beach that day. How many other innocent servants of the king lost their lives due to Lucio's treachery?

Lucio was responsible for the Wendover raid too. The harvest was over. What other reason could there be for the knights and soldiers to be dispatched to Wendover?

Cranston's death and his father's disappearance were due to the raid. Lucio knew how to come between April and he. *What is happening to April?* he thought.

Arno left him to rest and returned to his quarters. Brandyn could not sleep so after a while, he went on the ship's deck to think matters through.

Brandyn went to the back of the ship and found himself alone. He looked up at the scattered stars that peaked around the heavy clouds. It was cold. Brandyn looked across the foaming sea water and felt alone and helpless. He removed April's scarf and clasped it in his hand. He brought it to his face. The arome comforted him for the instance. Brandyn looked up toward the heavens and prayed.

"My Lord and My God, I beg you please protect April and her

family from any tyranny. Please restore my father to my mother and Meaghan."

Even as Brandyn prayed, he doubted for the safety of his loved ones. Since becoming a knight, which was his dream, matters were getting worse and worse. He was discouraged. He was losing what little hope he had. He looked out in the cold wind at the sea. The moon was full in the sky. He thought of one thing above all. Brandyn thought to himself, *what is happening to April?*

April is with Keveyn!

Author Biography

Born and raised in a northern Canadian town, the author did a lot of ice skating. He was educated at McMaster University while working in a grocery store. He met his wife while attending school, and both are blessed with two sons. He has sold life insurance and mutual funds for commission, did supply teaching when available and assisted with handicapped children. After returning to school, he finally achieved his lifelong dream of becoming a teacher and author. Of this book, the author was inspired by a bedtime story he made up for his son's birthday sleepover. The next year the same story was requested, but the author could not recall it exactly. So he was corrected every step of the way.

DATE DUE

OCT 0 9 2012

10 DEC 2013

Return Material Promptly